THE
BLUE
HOLE

THE BLUE HOLE

A BAHAMIAN SHORT STORY

BERTRAM SMITH

The Blue Hole
A Bahamian Short Story

ISBN: 978-1-950685-73-8

Printed in the United States of America

Dedicated to the children of the Bahamas—in the hope that they, too, will fall passionately in love with "stories" associated with our lands of birth, as I did growing up on the island of Andros.

FOREWORD

And They Will Say . . .
Tell us
Where you from again
And I will say
Andros
And they will laugh
An all too familiar laugh
And go
Andros . . .
And I will say
Yes
I am from Andros
I am from the island of Andros
Andros is home to me
Swimming in the Blue Hole
Running
Skipping
Playing
Frolicking
Skylarking with my friends along white sandy beaches
Yes, I am from the island of Andros
Andros is home to me
Andros

That sun-drenched land where it rains sometimes
In the summer time
And the coconut trees sway gently
In the swee cool breeze

What Mr. Smith has done, first in poetic form, in his collection *From the Puddle to the Pond*, and now in narrative form in the story of *The Blue Hole*, is to bring to life the sounds, the smells, the tastes, and most importantly, the people of The Bahamas.

While reading both works, I found myself transported and completely immersed in Mr. Smith's childhood home of the island of Andros. Mr. Smith's story, *The Blue Hole*, brings to the page a legend that will capture the imagination of everyone, young and old, both in his native Bahamas and the world beyond. It certainly resonated with this reader, a story-lover as well, from Cincinnati, Ohio, and made me dream of tropical ocean waves crashing onto pristine, sun-drenched beaches.

I have known Mr. Smith for over fifteen years. He is a man of faith, a family man, a consummate professional, colleague and mentor to the hundreds and hundreds of students who have had the honor (whether they knew it at the time or not) of being assigned to one of his language arts or social studies classes over the years.

In addition, I am proud to call Mr. Smith a friend. He is always available to provide wise counsel in all matters of life.

I hope you will keep these qualities in mind as you turn the pages of this fascinating book of realism and adventure. Knowing that the words emit from the heart and mind of such a man will only enhance the experience of your journey into *The Blue Hole*.

Michael Doyne
Educator
Director of Parent Center & Community
Outreach, Gwinnett County Public
Schools-LMS

Introduction

They are the perfect imperfect holes in the ground. They are the perfect secluded, secret get-away spots to go to and catch a refreshing bath. They are the perfect places to go sightseeing, or to swim or dive in. They are the perfect wonders, the sort of wonder that catches the eye, tickle the fancy, and excites the ever-curious scientific community. They are the perfect places to go, if you were a kid—like me—growing up in the Bahamas, in the good old days, and you wanted to get in trouble. And yes, they are the perfect sort of "stuff" that legends are born off. Like space travel, travel through time, sailing the deep blue yonder in centuries past, or descending into the mysterious deep dark blue, or landing on the moon or Mars.

The "they" are the now famous and world-renowned blue holes of the Bahamas.

If you have never experienced one of these unique geological formations that dot the physical landscape of the Bahamian islands, then you are missing out on one of history's—and science's—best kept secrets.

What are blue holes? And why do they still intrigue us? Why do we write stories about them? Blue holes, to put it simply, are gigantic holes in the ground that have filled up over a long period with a combination of fresh and saltwater. In essence, they are elaborate, ancient underwater caves and cave systems that nature has carved out of mostly coral and limestone rocks over the many centuries, both on land and in the sea. Historians and geologists believe that the existence of these watery phenomena extends all the way back as far as the ice age. They believe that the blue holes still hold treasures, secrets, to unlock the past.

There are hundreds of blue holes in the Bahamas. Most of them are located on the island of Andros, the largest island in the archipelago. Blue holes are scary, intimidating places—or at least they *were*, when I was growing up in the Bahamas. They were widely viewed as being beguilingly dangerous—much too dangerous, for example, to go swimming in.

Many stories had sprung up about the blue holes. Stories, for example, of how they were haunted; how strange creatures lived in their abyss; how the blue holes had no bottoms; or how many people had drowned or simply disappeared in the blue holes.

The many stories circulating about the blue holes, when I was coming up, had a more clearly defined and sinister purpose, it seemed. These many stories, we came to believe, were designed to frighten, as the "ole people" would say, the "dickens" or the daylight out of us young ones. The many stories were designed—or so we later came to believe—to keep us confined to the more "normal" channels of fun—running the white sandy beaches, swimming in the crystal-clear blue waters of the ocean, or fishing off one of the nearby jagged rocks that jutted out into the sea. These stories were so vintage and pervasively told—and believed—that many people who had lived their whole lives only a couple of stones' throw away had never experienced a blue hole.

I, myself, was about thirteen or fourteen when I first laid eyes on one—the one located less than a half of mile from where I was born and grew up in the settlement of Smith's Hill, South Andros. By the way, this blue hole is also the one that serves as part of the setting for the ensuing story. I will never forget the gripping sensation, the rush of adrenaline, and the awe that that swept over me the very first time I stood on the rocky ledge and took in the dreamy, silent, grandeur of the blue hole. The fact that

I was a child just made it more exaggeratingly stunning and grand.

As I have already intimated, after a while the blue hole became commonplace to us, mundane, just another place in our pantheon of places of adventures, places that we would frequent to escape the summer heat, to remove ourselves from the world of grownups and all the structures and strictures that their world engendered.

It never dawned on me that there was anything particularly special, historically unique about the blue holes. Over time, and as we grew older, the blue holes became just a part of our daily existence, much like the white sandy beaches, the clear blue crystal waters of the Atlantic, the gentle breeze, and the lazy sway of the branches of the coconut trees.

It was not until many years later after I had left the Bahamas that I began to muse and reflect on the blue hole and all of those dreadful, yet intriguing, stories. So you can probably imagine the thrill and amazement when I stumbled across a couple of articles in a National Geographic magazine about the blue holes of the Bahamas. Those articles, I thought to myself, were finally shining light into a part of *my* world—our world—that for so long had been shrouded in intellectual darkness and mystery. I couldn't help but take pride in the fact that science was finally shining a light into an all too familiar world—and confirming, at least snippets of the stories, I had grown up with!

Also surprising—and weirdly reassuring— were the artifacts the blue holes had yielded for inspection by a wildly excited scientific and intellectual community—ominous "treasures" such as stone axes and other rudimentary tools and—yes—even a human skull! I remembered thinking to myself, *Just maybe those "stories" were not so far-fetched after all.*

The perceptions of blue holes and the mystique that captivated us as kids are long gone now. Like almost everything else in the Bahamas and the wider Caribbean, they have become mild intellectual curiosities, must-see attractions for the millions of tourists that flock to our shores. They have become natural aquariums for visitors to "take in" as a next stop on their tours. Some visitors to the blue holes, professionals and semi-professional swimmers and divers, alike, are now content to swim, snorkel, and dive into their dark, cool, placid waters.

In the short story, The Blue Hole, I wanted to take the reader on a journey back to those enchanting times when I was growing up on the island of Andros. I wanted to allow this idyllic place and innocent time of my life to provide a platform, or launching pad, from which to escape into yet another world—a distant world, a world both far removed, yet reflective of the times in which we lived.

I started writing the short story, *The Blue Hole*, as a lengthy narrative poem to be included in my first offering, a partly autobiographical collection of poems/stories about growing up in the Bahamas and moving to the United States. I titled it, *From the Puddle to the Pond*. However, the more I labored over The Blue Hole, the more I came to realize that it was too massive and creepy a creature, that it was not malleable and moldable or given to the genre I was writing in. Furthermore, the story just kept growing and expanding into an even more sort of weird literary thing that I had little control over. That was when it dawned on me that it might be better off just letting it evolve and develop into a uniquely Bahamian short story/tale.

In retrospect, and after all these years, I have resigned myself to the idea that The Blue Hole, as a story, was—perhaps—meant, all along, to exist alone.

Table Of Contents

PROLOGUE

THE CHIEF, AN emaciated, yet authoritative-looking figure, strode slowly into the slightly dark room. The chief's white mustache and beard hung limply down in front of him, sweeping the dusty floor as he walked. As he walked, his mass of fingernails and toenails, like octopus' tentacles, writhed like snakes. The chief looked to be about three to four hundred years old, not a day younger. In his hand, he clutched a long slender pole, what looked—from the manner in which he carried it—like a kingly scepter. At the sight of which, I almost retched. I stumbled backwards. The sickness to my stomach that I had experienced earlier as I made my way up from the beach across the compound came flooding back. Impaled at the top of the ominous scepter was another decomposed human skull!

As scary as it was, the sight of his staff—or scepter—soon got lost in all of the pomp and pageantry that followed. All of the commotion and attention to detail was like the changing of the guard at Government House. It also reminded me of a scene from the story, King Arthur's Court. Except that in this strange, dark world, so far removed from anything we could call civilization, it all looked rather comical.

The old, wizened chief tapped with his one-of-a-kind scepter. The head atop the pole rattled and jiggled. All the other wizened and shriveled up creatures took a seat on the dark, dusty, and sandy floor. The chief tapped twice; the wizened, withered, wrinkled ones folded their arms. Then he tapped three more times and they all crossed their legs. Now, it all was beginning to look like the convening of a convention. However, we were quite happy and relieved when they all crossed their legs, because those skimpy pieces of loincloth they were wearing were becoming downright embarrassing.

The chief gave a series of loud taps with his ominous scepter. The impaled head that sat atop it shook and dangled precariously.

As I sat waiting—waiting for what, I did not know—I felt alone! Desperately alone. I had never felt so all alone in all my life! All I could do was sit on the dry, dusty, dark sand and fret about what was certain to be my most uncomfortable and unpleasant end. The Heads. In my mind's eye, I could see nothing but the heads, the lifeless, sockets for eyes and sallow cheekbones heads. The scalp-less heads. The piles and piles of DEAD and decomposed human skulls that greeted me when I entered the dusty, smoky compound, that adorned the place, came—along with that now familiar sickening, gut-wrenching feeling to my stomach—flooding back.

In the middle of my musing, ruminating, call it reflecting—much to my utter amazement—my three friends, their eyes still bulging from fright and shock, were ushered—not roughly, but not friendly, either—through the inner doorway, into the large room, rattling the seashell curtain once again. They looked haggard, bewildered, and in a daze. Like me, they too, must have thought they were in the middle of a nightmarish dream. Tears were streaming down my friends' cheeks. Their knees were shaking and knocking so hard, I could almost hear them from where I sat confused and dejectedly on the dark, sandy floor. The heads . . . Had they seen the heads too?

They—the strange, ghostly-looking creatures— had tied my friends' hands tightly behind their backs with some sort of reed.

I wanted to go to them, maybe try to console them—or, better yet, for us to console each other—but a set of grimy, long fingernails pressed down on my shoulder, digging deep into my flesh, causing me to wince with pain. I took that as a warning that I had better remain calmly seated.

The chief, like a master magician, raised his ominous scepter slowly, pointed it directly at my friends. His voice—the first time any of them had spoken—rang out like garrulous thunder, rattled throughout the hut, and rolled and floated through the coconut trees, bouncing of the tops of the coca plum bushes out onto the bay, and barreled down the dark deserted beach.

To our utter amazement, the chief spoke English. In a voice that also sounded like thunder, he shouted in a loud voice, "Loose them, and let them go!"

CHAPTER 1

THE FORBIDDEN PLACE

OUR PARENTS HAD warned us. They had warned us good, as the people say. They had warned us a million times.

"Stay away!"

"You hear me?"

"Don't go there! Don't even go near that place!"

"I don't *ever* want to hear 'bout you going 'round there, you understand?"

"And if I ever catch you—or *even* hear 'bout you goin' 'round there…"

At which point their voices would trail off. They didn't have to finish that particular sentence, for we already *knew* what they would do. And the tamarind tree that sat just atop the hill from our house would wink and say, *"How do you do?"*

Then, on the heels of all the warnings, would come the stories, stories we had heard a million times, stories that made you suddenly bolt upright in bed in the middle of the night in a cold-hot sweat. Stories about how it was too dangerous; how, "it had been reported"—on numerous occasions—that, strange things happened there—especially late at night. It was even "believed" that strange creatures lived there. Some claimed to have heard the strange sounds emanating from the spot, very late at night, when the moon was full, and it was calm and no wind was blowing. They said the sounds were sad, haunting sounds, like someone crying or moaning—or singing intoxicating songs, songs that nobody "could make out."

The stories would sometimes branch out, in an implicating, threatening sort of way, to include children, children just like us, who had not heeded their parent's stern warnings and had gone swimming there, and had either drowned or disappeared, never to be heard from again.

And so the stories went—the stories of the infamous blue hole. And this was how they—the stories—grew—and grew—*and grew*—and became crystalized into island legends—even if only in our imaginations and in our imaginings of them.

The stories were poignant and convincingly real, too. They conjured up in us this dark and mysterious place where the water was so dark you couldn't even see your hands and feet under the water. They summoned up images of strange creatures, terrifying creatures, or maybe chickcharneys that we had all heard about. Or even mermaids, sliding, gliding, slithery-like, smoothly and effortlessly across the jagged limestone rocks to sit and bathe late at night, then easing themselves back into the cool, dark waters.

As far as we knew, no fish lived in the blue hole. In all our "born days," as the old folks would say, we had never seen or heard of anyone going fishing there.

As to why no fish lived in the blue hole was itself an open question. Like the stories about the blue hole, stories as to why no fish lived there abounded. Some said the waters of the blue hole was simply too muddy. Not enough oxygen. They said that even if fish wanted to live there, they wouldn't be able to see through the dark cloudy water, or breathe the thick murky water through their sensitive gills. Others said that the waters of the blue hole, unlike the water in the sea, was not salty enough for the fish's taste. Yet others opined that *whatever* it was that lived in the blue hole had more than likely gobbled up everything that once lived and thrived there.

Something else they said. They said that not even birds would fly directly over the blue hole.

According to the reports, birds—gaulins and other long-necked cranes, pigeons, wood doves, tobacco doves, song birds, and even chim chims would be flying, and—all of a sudden—lay eyes on the blue hole, and immediately file a new flight plan, come to a screeching halt in the sky, turn, tip their wings, respectfully, and proceed to go around.

Growing up in Andros, the old folks use to always laugh and say how animals—especially birds—were much "smarter than people," how they could smell a storm, or an impending danger, or disaster, long before it struck.

When we were young, the stories were enough to make our hair stand on ends. We had all grown up with the stories. The stories were part of our daily existence. They were as much a part of our lives as the sermons my dad would preach on Sunday mornings—or, like the stories my mom would share with us as she leaned on her broom in the middle of the already immaculate "dining room," stories she had told us a thousand times before.

The stories about the blue hole, though, had penetrated deep down into our souls in a dull, vague sort of way, just enough to control us, keep us, as they say, from not venturing off the straight and narrow way.

The stories were not your typical old-time Bahamian folktale, either. They were nothing like the "Bruh Bookie and Bruh Rabbie" stories we had grown up with. These "old time" stories, about two cantankerous, dim-witted characters from a distant, sketchy past, were intended mainly for laughs and poking fun. They were reserved for those times spent whiling the time away late at night, when we were gathered around an open fire roasting corn.

Sometimes we would tell the Bruh Bookie and Bruh Rabbie stories on steamy hot "slow nights" when "crab wasn't walkin'," or, at other times when our bags were so full of the delectable crustaceans, that we needed an occasional respite from the long trek back home and the weight of the overflowing bags. The Bruh Bookie and Bruh Rabbie stories made for great late-night entertainment, light jocular humor to lighten up the often-prevailing dark and brooding mood that could accompany "goin' crabbin." Even our—for the most part—sullen and no-nonsense parents would have to crack up and smile at the end of one of those "foolish" and "crazy" stories.

The stories about the blue hole, however, were quite different. They were riveting, emotionally exhaustive—and purposeful. Their pointed intention—one that worked for a long time—was to just reach out and grab ahold of every fiber in our tiny frames and rattle us to the core. Our parents would tell the stories about the blue hole with a certain degree of aplomb, as if they were rooted in age-old fact, as if they were certifiably verifiable, even with names attached to them as witnesses to their veracity. No one found it a tad bit odd in the slightest that all of the subjects linked to these stories had either left the island a long time ago or had "departed this earth."

Yes, our parents had warned us mus'be a gazillion times. And they had skillfully seasoned the warnings with the stories. They didn't just warned us, either. They strictly forbade us to "even look in the direction" of the blue hole. After all the warnings—and the stories—you could say that the blue hole, was our tree in the middle of the garden.

CHAPTER 2

WHEN "THE FORBIDDEN" KEEPS CALLING OUT YOUR NAME

GROWING UP ON the island of Andros, we had heard all of the stories. As time went by, however, the stories began to lose their grip on us. We began to see them in a slightly different light, with a little less palpability. We still believed in the stories. They still had some tug on our minds and our souls, lurking somewhere in the corners of our collective consciousness. However, as time went on, they began to lose some of their powerful sway over our lives.

Now, we were beginning to view many of the stories from the perspective of a ploy. Possible concoctions. Designed—maybe—just maybe—as a form of parental conceit and deceit, a community conspiracy, even ingenuity.

Perhaps, went the whispers between us, they—the stories—were nothing more than a tactic, a device, a tool to keep us as far away as possible from what our wise and sage old ancestors knew would lure us away from the normal channels of fun.

We were beginning to think like our parents, put ourselves in their shoes. Which all brought us to the conclusion that, maybe they thought, if we were to ever experience the blue hole, taste it—just maybe—it would be the end of all they had so carefully and skillfully crafted to keep us "safe and sound, and out of trouble."

We also knew that, after all, one of the first rules of parents—at least, that was how it was with parents when we were growing up in Andros—was to keep us kids out of the house at whatever cost. They did not want us either "messin' up the house," or, as my mom would say, "eatin' up the whole house."

And since they couldn't keep their eyes on us *all* of the time, or track our *every* movement, maybe the warnings, combined with all of the stories, were just their way of hemming us in, building a hedge of protection around us, controlling where we went, where we drifted, where we wandered, and where we roamed.

We eventually came around to one conclusion—and that is, that our parents needed all of that skill and ingenuity to keep us out of the house, and, at the same time, as much as possible, not too far from their roving eyes.

Again, all of the stories were enough to scare us, rattle and disturb us to the core. However, the one that really unnerved us and sent chills rippling up and down our spines, was the one that said the blue hole had no bottom. That right there—was enough to make us stop whatever we were doing, sit up, and take note. *Had no bottom!* Had no bottom? Who had ever heard of such a thing, we would shrug? Everything had a bottom—or so at least we thought. After all, there was a bottom to the Eel Pond; there was a bottom to the sea, the deepest part of it. In school, we had learned that even the ocean had a bottom, and that fish and crabs and many other creatures lived on the ocean's floor. Thus, to say that something did not have a bottom—now that right there, like I said, was designed to really mess, with our young, impressionable minds. *And* it did, too! At least for a while.

The story about the blue hole, how it was a virtual watery graveyard, how it did not have any bottom, how only bad things happened there, did rule our lives for a while. For the longest, we just could not get it out of our minds, no matter how hard we tried. Playing stickball in the crossroad with old stuff socks and a piece of stick, we would be thinking about it; running wildly on the long stretch of white sandy beach, we would still be thinking about how the blue hole had no bottom. Even at school, trying to read "Dick and Jane," and how they chased Spot over the meadow, the thought of the blue hole having no bottom would intervene between the pages. And we would see Spot, running freely—blurry-like—and wildly, with reckless abandon, missing his step, stumbling and tumbling, falling straight into the blue hole—falling, tumbling, tumbling down, down, maybe, all the way back to England.

CHAPTER 3

ONE DAY YOU ARE HAPPY, THE NEXT, YOU ARE . . .

MY DAD, WHO liked to say—admonish us—mind y'all stay out of dem people yard; don't y'all have y'all own yard to play up in—said, So, y' all bored, eh? I'll tell you what—this is Andros—this ain't nothing like Nassau. There is plenty of open spaces here. I'll tell you what y'all can do. You can go out on the bay. Out there, you can walk the beach all day long, my dad said. Go south. Go north. Walk south as far as you can go until you can't walk any further. Then turn around and walk the other way. (The bay—when we talked about "the bay"—represented everything from the wide, open expanse of blue sky, sparkling emerald green and blue sea, the long stretches of white sandy beach, the slightly dark canopy of the coconut groves, to nearby "bottoms" of sugar cane that rustled and waved in the cool, sweet breeze under the hot tropical sun).

So this—what my dad said—sounded, to us, like fun, sheer unadulterated fun and freedom! However, we had missed the humor or the "catch" in his voice when he had first said it. We took him up on his challenge one day.

Back then, we did not have the foggiest idea how long Andros was, or how wide, for that matter. We did not know, for example, that South Andros alone was a big chunk of land. All we knew was that it prescribed and sufficed all of our needs. We had never thought in terms of miles—only in terms of opportunity and adventure—new opportunities and new adventures to slay the fits of boredom.

So that day we walked up and down the beach, skimming stones, digging in the sand, splashing in the crystal-clear waters as we went. We would splash endlessly through the clear water—the sunlight hitting and shimmering off the water—scattering schools of shads and narrow shads whenever they would appear like dark clouds gliding stealthily just beneath the surface of the water, playing as we went—just plain old skylarking.

Then there were the whitish-greyish sand crabs that would scamper swiftly across the beach in zigzag fashion, whenever they saw us approaching, and, in the blink of an eye, would dive, squeeze, quickly, headfirst, into their tiny holes, their secret underworlds, to escape our careless marching feet. We did not think much of these small, innocent, sand crabs. To us, the only thing they were good for was squashing and mushing beneath our chomping feet, or smashing them away with a piece of stick, the way we swatted at the ball when we played stickball in the crossroad. However, to them, we must have seemed like selfish, unsympathetic, cruel trespassers—uncaring invaders, who were un-phased and unmindful of their way of life. So they would dash for the hatches whenever they saw an intruder coming, leaving their peaceful and idyllic world above for a less desirous sanctuary deep down below.

We found all sorts of interesting "treasures" washed up on the shore and on the rocks as we walked, ran, and spun along the way. Tangled up in the seaweeds, we found a dead shark. The flies were buzzing, and a few crows (buzzards) were already hovering, circling. We chased them away, paulting them with rocks. But they were crafty and stubborn buggers. They just dodged, glided, and stalled just above the reaches of our projectiles. We finally gave up the fight, realizing we were encroaching on their territory, preventing them from doing their jobs.

Old shoes, all kinds of bottles—the kind Cousin Irene hung from the branches of her fruit trees in her yard that cast a spell on all the fruits, that caused us kids much fear and trepidations—and containers littered the ground. Some of the stuff washed ashore, we had no idea what they were. Discarded items from passing ships, no doubt. Old pieces of plastics and plastic bags. We started collecting them. That is, until we realize the futility in that, so we just kept walking, half-running.

Then one of us would break the silence. They would say what we all were thinking that there ought to be a law against all the plastic washing up on our otherwise beautiful, clean beaches. "Yeah, there oughta be a law," someone else chimed in. Then Picewell would say, "Maybe we should report the matter to the governor,"—and we would all chase after him across the white boggy sand and pummel him for being so out of character with the whole vibe and mood of the moment. The governor—yeah, right! Who had ever seen the governor in Andros, we thought.

We had left home bright and early, reached the top of the southern end of Andros sometime around noon. We stood there for a while, let out a yell, jammed a piece of stick with an old plastic bag for a flag in the ground to mark our conquest, then turned around and headed north. We were going to show my dad! How dare he? How dare he dare us to walk the length of the island? Did he not know that this was our island? Yes, this was our kingdom—and we were the kings of it!

We were all thinking that, maybe, if we conquered the island—at least the entire length of it—that would be it; there would be nothing left to subdue. Then we all thought it the same time—blurted it out—in unison: "The blue hole!"

We slapped palms, spat in our hands, wiped our shirtfronts clean in an act comradery and solidarity, and kept on pushing into the slight head wind. A newfound energy and elation propelling us.

The first fifty or so miles were easy, even fun. Then fatigue started to set in. The sun started beating down on us burning and stinging our bare backs. We had tucked our shirts in our pockets, draped them over our shoulders, or just let them hang flopping from our hands now.

We were also too tired to kick any more sand. Soon our mouths were starting to feel dry and parched. Our legs were beginning to feel heavy, like lead, from trudging through the boggy sand. When we would come to the rocky areas, we would tiptoe lightly and quickly over the jagged coral and limestone rocks. Shoes had not yet become fashionable in Andros.

We discovered water by the Drain, a natural spring that came bubbling out of the ground and over the smooth rock ledge. Slurping and gurgling, we drank thirstily and shoved off again. However, by the time we reached the Bluff settlement we decide to turn around. There were no long stretches of beaches in this direction, not like in Kemp's Bay and Smith's Hill. Only jagged rocks, pocked marked with puddles, jutting out into the sea. Some of these giant rocks loomed large and high reminding us of jagged cliffs we had seen in storybooks. In certain spots, the waves would come crashing against the rocks, with resounding and recurring rhythm, rhythms like pounding, dull drumbeats, sending showers of sprays spewing powerfully into the air as the rocks inhaled and exhaled like whales.

We made it home just before dusk. My mom and dad were sitting on the porch listening to the evening news on their transistor radio. My dad had that wry smile on his face that we had all come to know too well.

"You boys back so soon? How did it go?"

It was *all right*, we said wearily and dejectedly, realizing, for the first time, that my dad had tricked us—no, he had duped us, and he had duped us good! We had completely exhausted ourselves just the way he had envisioned and planned it. He had found the cure—or so he thought—for a couple of kids who suffered with boundless energy, and who were always complaining about being bored.

That night, our parents did not have to usher us off to bed as they usually did. And the big pot of crab-and-dough sitting atop the stove, the ultimate island dinner treat, did not seem all that enticing to us, either. We were "dog-tired," as they say, and we drifted off to sleep as soon as our heads hit the pillows.

We may have drifted off to sleep, but the thoughts of the blue hole did not leave us. They flitted in and out of our dreams. In our dreams, we saw gaulins and other long-necked cranes flapping their wings furiously and shrieking, "Beware the blue hole! Beware the blue hole!"

CHAPTER 4

SOMETIMES, THE BACK-STORY JUST CANNOT WAIT UNTIL THE END

IT FELL TO reason, then, that we could have easily blamed our parents—and their parents, before them—for what happened to us on that fateful day, that one hot lazy summer day in July. They should never have told us that the blue hole—what we had come to believe just might be the greatest, yet-to-be-discovered adventure of them all—was "strictly forbidden."

Thus, it was really no surprise—or, at least, it shouldn't have been any surprise—when, on that day, a really hot summer day, there we were—Picewell, Toney, Lawrence, and me, headed straight for the dreaded, and, what we had come to believe, was the the much maligned blue hole!!

It must have been part fate, too. I don't know where we summoned up the courage. Who was it that said there is a thin line between courage and being foolish? We would not have known, because they obviously were not talking to us. All I knew was that it was hot that day, real hot—grimy and sticky hot, so hot, the sweat was pouring off our thin, scraggly bodies and causing our raggedy shirts and shorts to cling. Besides, as everyone knows, it gets hot in Andros, so hot that, apart from causing sunstroke, the heat could really start to mess with one's mind.

Picewell, Toney, and Lawrence—they were my friends, my constant companions, my running-buddies, my fellow conquistadors. We had grown up in the same settlement, and we were family—do not ask me how. There are some things, since they cannot be explained, are just best left alone. However, suffice it to say, we did everything together—shooting marbles and spinning tops in the middle of the road in defiance of the few cars and trucks that sometimes came rumbling and barreling through. The irate drivers—all of them "Cousin Something" or "Another"—would yell at us to get out of the street, demanding to know if we were "out of our minds or just trying to get killed." Often, when the sun was going down, and it was getting cool, we would play stickball in the crossroad with a piece of stick and old stuffed socks. Everyone passing by on the nearby main road could hear us yelling loudly and vociferously about whether a pitch was a "ball" or "strike," or whether someone had been "tagged" out or had managed to elude the tag.

These games were intense; and would last for as long as we could see the "ball," or until one of our parents would yell in their distinctive voice for us to come home. At other times, we would summon the courage and get our adrenalines flowing by scaling our neighbors' fences or walls to raid their mango, guenep, or guava trees. Then we would run pell-mell down the beach, kicking and punching one another and gorging ourselves on the sweet, delicious fruits.

We—that is to say—Tony, Picewell, Lawrence, and me—had shared many adventures—and misadventures—together. Like the time when Lawrence came running over to our house with a pamelly bump in the back of his head that was sticking out the size of a shiny, ripe dilly, that looked like it was still growing. He had had the nerves to say to his mom, Cousin Tella (Esthella, but everyone we knew called her Tella), that he wasn't going to take any more "whuppin'," something completely unheard of *ever* in the annals of Andros history. No kid, no kid that is, who wanted to walk away with his life, live to see another day, would dare to say to their parents that they were not going to take any more beatings—not any parent in the Andros that we knew growing up. Lawrence was dead meat from the start!

"'Lisha and Bertram don't get whuppins no more. And I ain't takin' no more either!"

Now whoever had told Lawrence that lie—about my brother and I, not being on the receiving end of a belt or a tamarind switch anymore—was flat out lying to him—or simply did not have his best interest at heart.

This was back in the day when we use to have "shooters," or hunters, come down to Andros. They were mostly white, affluent Bahamian men—the Gumps, Solomons, Pinders, and Kellys. They were famous shooters, known for their pigeon-shooting skills; they could bring a bunch of white-crowned pigeons down out the clear blue yonder with one volley of shots. Cousin Tella, was a far better shooter than all of them, in our humble opinion. When Lawrence said that to his mom, the only one he knew, the one that brought him into this world and who had nursed and burped him—from the moment he said what he said, he was good as dead. That was when Cousin Tella's hand just whipped out, came to rest on the nearest object, cocked, and fired—she was a lefty too—and brought Lawrence down with a thud just like one of them white-crowned pigeons. Her weapon—one of those giant can of beans, the kind you buy at the A-Wong store in Nassau.

My other life-long friend, Tony, was an irrepressible kid with boundless energy who loved to make the girls laugh on the way home from school. Tony was a daredevil. He was the only kid we knew who would dare scale the old half-broken-down rock wall to steal fruits from Cousin Irene's yard. That is until his bravery and bravado almost cost him his life.

Everyone knew that Cousin Irene was one of a kind. She was a recluse who kept to herself, living in the shadows of the countless fruit trees that almost obscured her house from the road. Everyone also knew that Cousin Irene had her yard "fixed." All of the lovely fruit trees bore on them the distinctive marks of death—a regalia of colorful bottles that dangled and danced in the cool breeze. And it was precisely because of us kids that Cousin Irene had resorted to this drastic measure. From the looks of those carefully and artfully decorated trees, there was not a doubt in this world that her intentions, evil as they were, were to make us think twice before scaling her wall. The fruits on those trees—on the one hand, screamed at every kid who passed, "See me; see how sweet I am!"—and, on the other hand, they screamed, "Eat me and you will die!" So all of us kids, out of much respect as much as dread, knew how to walk on the other side of the road whenever we passed by Cousin Irene's yard and look the other way.

Cousin Irene's yard was more like an orchard or wild garden, and, she lived there with her old blind husband, who we never saw, and a pack of "pot-cake" dogs that barked all the time. Cousin Irene's pot-cakes would bark at anything. They barked for their food, they barked at any—and all—passerby; they barked whenever Cousin Irene came out of the house; they barked if the wind so much as blew too hard.

Cousin Irene was strange. She kept to herself and never talked to anyone. Once-in-a-while, we would see her peering out from behind a semi-dark giant leaf or grapefruit, the sunlight streaming throughout the well shaded yard. It was not clear to us whether she had any family. No one ever came from Nassau or the States to visit Cousin Irene.

The bottles didn't just adorn *some* of the fruit trees, either. Hanging from *every* tree in Cousin Irene's yard was a messaged-filled, ominous-looking bottle. They were an array of colorful bottles she had collected from off the bay and carefully hung from every branch of every tree. They were of all different sizes, shapes, and colors too. She had collected them during her routine and bright-and-early walks out on the bay with her pack of jumping, barking pot-cakes. These ominous objects dangled and did a slight dance in the cool breeze. The dangling, swaying bottles were "protection" from anyone who dared enter her yard to steal one of her fruits.

And no one dared enter Cousin Irene's yard to steal one of those fruits, either. We just knew that if the snarling pot-cakes did not get you, whatever she had in those strange bottles would. Cousin Irene had gone to a whole heap of trouble to ward off us "rotten" kids. From every branch—and every limb—she had carefully, and meticulously, hung her bottles of death!

None of us would even dare think of entering her yard, much less touch a fruit from off of one of her fruit trees. None of us, that is, except Tony! One fateful day, Tony—either because it was very hot that day, or, because he wanted to show off in front of the girls, stopped, cleared everyone else out of his path with a series of motions with his arms, and said: "Get out of the way!" and "Watch this!" He kicked off a few times with his legs as if to gain traction—and he was off like a rocket! We all watched, aghast, as Tony, in one deft motion, scaled Cousin Irene's rock wall. (Cousin Irene's wall, the rocks carefully and skillfully laid eons ago, was a story unto itself.)

The dogs did not even have time to react to Tony, when he catapulted over that wall just like a cannon ball. Either the potcakes didn't have time to react, or, they couldn't believe anyone could be so foolish to even consider such a feat. Tony was back in a flash, too! He was hugging and clutching his trophies—at least a half dozen big ole juicy yellow-orange mangoes. The girls all ooohed and giggled in stunned disbelief, their hands cupping their mouths sheepishly. Tony proudly displayed his—to us—very questionable trophies—munched on them as we watched, filled with awe and trepidations. He offered some to us. We all shook our heads violently and said, "Uhh-uhhn, that's alright!" However, from that moment forth, the careful and sly watch was on to see how long it would take for Tony to drop down dead.

The next day we all learned that Tony was at home, sick as a dog. He was on his dying bed, some said. They reported, with much solemnity, that if we wanted to see Toney, we had better go quick, because Tony's life "could be hanging by a thread." They had no idea how much longer he could manage to hold on. Reports also had it that he was already "talking out of his head," seeing visions of long-lost relatives and angels, and losing and regaining consciousness. From all accounts, he was in a bad way, probably nearing the fatal end. All because of Cousin Irene's yard, which, we all were convinced was the sure kiss of death.

From the main road, we could hear Tony wailing and hollering. Sometimes he would wail and holler; sometimes his voice would just come and go in a moan like someone singing a sad, sad song.

His house was at the end of a long, winding, weed-filled down-the-middle path, lined with some cedar trees. Cousin Izzie (Elizabeth), the woman, we all knew as his grandmother, directed us to the back of the house because she would not have anyone "t'ramplin'" through her living room, messing it up. We stood on our tippy-toes and peered through the window into Tony's small, disheveled room where he was balled-up, clutching at his stomach—he was in one of his wailing and hollering phases—and he was calling on everybody he knew—or thought— could help him, including his Mammie, His Grand-Mammie, long lost relatives, Jesus, and God. In desperation, he had even called out our names a couple of times. We looked at each other, frowned, and crinkled up our noses and thought the same thing the same time, *"Man, whatever Cousin Irene had put in those bottles must have been some serious mojo!"*

Tony obviously survived that scare.

Picewell, was my other best friend. Picewell was more like a younger brother to me, always by my side, and a constant partner anytime we played stickball in the crossroad with old stuffed socks. Picewell and I, as they say, just saw eye to eye on everything.

So there we were, striking out on a new path that day, charting our own course, one might say, on our way to unlocking one of the best kept secrets in Andros' history—and perhaps—just perhaps—living out one of the greatest adventures of our young lives.

It began, as it always did, it seemed—hot, sunny day, looking to find something to do, something to up the ante, some way to escape the summer heat. I cannot remember whose idea it was, but it must have sounded good to all of us—because there we were. Yes, there we were, walking briskly, all nervous and excited, being pulled, dragged, toward the spot as if by some strange, mysterious magnetic force, headed directly for the blue hole, the dreaded, and—what we had come to believe—a much maligned blue hole!

We walked determinedly, resolutely, not bothering to talk. After all, there was nothing to say—no time for conversation—through the bushes, slapping at the mosquitoes—small, insignificant, yet constant nemeses—tearing at the bushes slapping us in the face. Even the thick jungle of vines and chinnie-briars were no match for us that day. We tore through them as if they were nothing. Nervous and all excited—all at the same time—our hearts pumping and racing a thousand miles a minute, we pushed through, like a small rag-tag army of young explorers, looking for that place where we could, for once and for all, claim and plant our flag.

CHAPTER 5

A SIMPLE GAME OF HIDE-AND-SEEK LEADS TO A WILD ADVENTURE

OUR HEARTS WERE really pumping and thumping that day. After walking for what seemed like an eternity through the bush, brushes, and wild thicket, we stumbled into a rocky clearing. That was when we first laid eyes on it. The blue hole. The view, like a picture in a frame, it just rushed into view, slapping us smack in the faces, causing us to stumble backwards, gawking at the view we had found. Unforgettable moments—they can sometimes come in the form of a photograph; they can come in the form of a postcard—or, they could come in the form of what lay sprawling before us!

There it was—the blue hole! Like a brave new world all to itself. Nothing like we had ever seen—or imagined! The largest, most massive watery place we had ever laid eyes on—except, maybe, not counting the ocean. The first thing that struck us was the sheer grandeur of it. Next, was the peaceful calm, calm all around, then the rocky jagged walls and jagged ledges sprung into view, ghostly looking, bare bleached out and weathered limestone rocks! Beyond the rocks, and to the west, were the thick forests and the tall, stately looking, pine trees for as far as the eyes could see. To the east, and tapering off to the beach and the sea, were the thick, low-lying jungle of matted grey-green-and-yellow mangroves, lilies, punctuated with yellow elder flowers.

What caught our attention the most, however, was the dark, murky, and mysterious-looking water—the dark, murky, and mysterious-looking water that seemed to be hiding some carefully kept, just as dark and mysterious secret.

To us, the blue hole and its surroundings just looked like one big ole giant, watery paradise. It was quiet. No. It was scarily and eerily quiet. The blue hole—the first time our eyes feasted on it—looked stunningly peaceful, both real and surreal. Strangely enough, it also looked alluring and dangerously-excitingly inviting. In fact, it looked like it was just calling, beckoning to us, calling out to us like in Ulysses and the Sirens.

When we first saw it, hidden where it was in the "back-a da-bush," the thick forest, our hearts skipped a few beats, went aflutter. There are those times, when it just seems as if, all of nature, its symphony—a cacophony of sounds—like a wobbly record, just stops! Holds its breath, waiting to exhale again. This was one of those moments. We just knew that our day—a new day of discovery—had finally arrived.

Hidden where it was—you couldn't see the Blue Hole from the road. And if you did not know it was there, you could just walk right pass it. Hidden from view by a combination of boulders, rocks, trees, a tangle mass of vines and shrubs. It was that protected, that much of a well-kept secret. Not anymore! We had uncovered the treasure, and we just could not wait to dive into its deep, dark unknown.

We gasped, laughed nervously, started slapping, punching, and pummeling one another with glee, Andros-boy style. Tony let out a sudden and wild shriek for no reason, howling like an excited wild potcake. He certainly knew how to do the unexpected. It was exciting and scary how our voices just echoed out over the peaceful waters, up against the high rocks and pine trees, and floated away. We felt like we had entered a new world, a new world that had, just like that, crashed, in a beautiful sort of way, our, for the most part, ordinary and mundane world.

The Blue Hole, surrounded by jagged cliffs, marshes, and a thick mass of tangled mangroves, was nothing like we had ever seen before, nor like anything we had envisioned. It actually looked like what one would imagine a well-watered, wild, and luscious garden to look like. The only difference was that right smack in the middle of our pristine and luscious wild garden, was the largest swimming hole we had ever seen. It could have easily been confused for a lake. However, growing up in Andros, we had never seen a real lake before, so we had no idea what one was, or would even look like.

We simply could not believe the breathtaking view and the feeling that washed over us, a feeling of calmness, a feeling of wanting to stay right there, never to be bothered again with the rigors and rigidness that encumbered our world of the settlement. The blue hole—it was just like a living, breathing, shiny, shimmering, enormous, wild, and mammoth, but beautiful monster, in the middle of nowhere! It was scary. Like it was privy to some secrets we did not know. We could not help but noticed a few tiny ripples even tickling and disturbing the surface of the otherwise still, dark waters.

We could not peel our clothes off fast enough. Somebody pushed somebody. Then somebody pushed somebody else. Before we knew it, we were all shrieking, splashing, spitting, bobbing up and down in the cool, refreshing, and delightful waters.

It is strange how, when you are a kid, fear just seems to lose its sway in numbers, just float, scoot, and melt, away. How, at times, you can come down with a sudden case of amnesia, even temporary insanity. Our parents, their voices, their warnings, the stories—all just flew the coop as soon as we made that first loud splash, cracking the surface of the dark and murky waters. What we saw—the only thing we saw—was opportunities—the boundless fun and endless possibilities of our newfound watery paradise.

If this would have been a shindig, down in Louisiana style, then you could say the band was playing, the music thumping, the roof and walls were clapping, and we were kicking up our heals!

We swam, dived, splashed water at each other, and even did forward and backward summersaults. Then came the splashing and slapping of the water and some more shrieking. We would crawl up out of the water quickly, scramble and scamper across the jagged limestone rocks, and from as high as we could climb, dive, headfirst, into the cool, dark, now well-disturbed waters.

Our parents were right about one thing. You simply could not see any bottom—not even close. You could not even see your hands and legs under the water. I must admit, that was a little bit scary and unnerving at first. What if one of those creatures they had warned us about just came stealthily at first, then leaped up—loudly and ferociously from below—breaking the intensely delicious silence, and grabbed one of us and would let go?

For much of the time we just treaded water. When we had dove, we had not come near to touching anything that remotely felt like bottom. But we were all expert swimmers. Growing up in Andros took care of that. It was something we prided ourselves on.

In the summertime, in order to escape, to find relief from the hot days of summer, we would practically live on the beach and in the ocean—swimming, splashing and threshing around, chasing and burying each other's heads underwater for the count.

Sometimes we would venture far out to sea, far from the other laughing, squealing, and shrieking younger kids. And in the strangely peaceful and quiet deep water, we would dive for conchs or spear crawfish, hogfish, and snappers with homemade spears.

Then, at other times, we would run out onto the bay—just in time—to catch the local fishermen, pushing their small dinghies off from the shore, heading out to sea in search of their daily catch. And we would steal rides, holding on to the sterns of the boats for as long as we could, or, until the fishermen discovered we were there. When they did, they would jab and slap at us playfully with their oars, to dislodge us, causing us to lose our firm grips.

Sometimes, when we would turn around to look back toward the shore, the kids playing along the shoreline would look like little, tiny specs in the water.

So having to stay constantly afloat in the mysteriously dark, murky waters of the blue hole was no problem for us. In fact, it was a part of the game, part of the challenge, part of the excitement, part of what made it so much fun.

We played and splashed around for no telling how long. We would race across half of its width, shove each other's heads far under the water for the count, and even play tag. We came to discover that birds did fly over the blue hole. Every so often, a few gaulins, or some other type of long-necked crane, would drift overhead, screeching and cawing hysterically. Sometimes, their loud broken cries, coming from the sky above, in the otherwise peaceful, quiet surrounding, would catch us off guard, startling us. The cries, breaking the otherwise peaceful air, would seem quite ominous, as if they were trying to warn us of *an* impending danger.

After swimming, diving, threshing around, racing, chasing each other, and jumping from the jagged cliffs as many times as we could tolerate, we had had enough of that. That is when one of us suggested that we play hide-and-seek—a simple game of hide and seek. What could go wrong with that? The idea was for everyone—except one—to dive and hide in the dark murky waters and let the others find you.

As it turned out, I was "it." The others swam out quickly near the middle, plunged in, and disappeared from view.

For a fleeting moment, all was quiet and still. Just for a quick flash, being all alone, it frightened me. I could not help but think, "What if my friends never came back, never resurfaced?"

In a big open space like the one we were in—quiet—just for a split second—a touch of dread can take ahold of you, shake you, and rattle you. That is when the voices came drifting back. I started thinking about the stories. The stories and the warnings. I started thinking about the other kids—those, who maybe had not heeded the stern warnings. I heard the crowded, tumultuous voices of our parents reverberating inside my head.

People have disappeared in the blue hole!
The blue hole is no place for children!

And If I ever catch you even going near that place . . .

Stay away from there, you hear!

Stay away! Stay away! Stay away!

I shook myself free from the moment, the distracting, immobilizing, and depressing thoughts. Could not be bothered with those right now. I said to the spot where I had last seen my friends,

"Okay! Ready or not, I'm coming to find you!"

CHAPTER 6

WHAT HAPPENED NEXT IS ONE FOR THE BOOKS

I SHUT MY EYES, clenched them tight, and dove in. Then I opened them again, trying to look around, through the dark and murky waters. All was dark, muddy dark, like being inside of a dark shadowy cave. I felt around, spinning in all directions. That was when it hit me—this was not going to be easy. I started flailing my arms and poking around. But no matter how much I probed, poked, juked and flailed around in the dark waters with my arms, my friends were nowhere to be found!

I decided to come up for a quick spell. Nervous and all excited, breathing hard and fast, I gasped, took one big loud draught of fresh air, and plunged in again. I swam a little deeper. I flailed my arms and hands around wildly again, trying to touch one of my friends. No such luck.

If this *would have been* a shindig, then you could say this was where the music came to a screeching halt—just froze—and reality, unpleasant, ugly reality stepped in and arrested everything.

I started to panic! I swam deeper. Flailed around some more. Bubbles and sounds were escaping from my mouth and nostrils. It was like a dull symphony of noise now, what sounded like loud noises, inside my head. I yelled out my friends' names. My screams were just muffled, dull and soggy. I swam deeper still, thinking to myself, they must be around here somewhere. I swam-dived, twirled, deep beneath the surface for as long as I could hold my breath, spinning and thrashing around in the deep, dark, murky waters. Confused and dazed, I tried to think.

Should I go back, or should I go on? How much farther could I go? I couldn't go back. Too far. A dull beam of sunlight like the beam of an old, beat up flashlight covered in mud was all I could make out. Just a little bit farther, I told myself. My head started to swell. I swam and swam. I was beginning to lose track of time. How long had I swam, or to what depth? My only focus—and burning desire—was finding, and touching, one of my friends.

Disoriented, and without knowing it now, I kept on swimming. Without realizing it, I started to tumble, hurtle—going down, down, fast, faster, faster still. I was plummeting down, down. It felt like a watery abyss. I struggled to control myself, to gain my balance, get control of myself. However, something like a strong whoosh-whoosh, a dull sucking, engulfing, enveloping swoosh was sucking me in, pulling me down, causing me to career out of control. I chortled-screamed for help. However, the loud whooshing, gurgling, belching, muffling sound was all that I could hear.

Panic is something sudden, arresting. It sends your heart on an excursion, that makes it flutter wildly, that leads to internal confusion that leads to that pounding chaos in your chest. Those were the strange, yet familiar sensations that grabbed ahold of all of my defenseless members, now. I found myself yelling, calling on everyone I knew or thought could help me, starting with my parents, then my grandparents, my favorite aunts and uncles, even those long dead and gone, and ending with the Virgin Mary, the angel Gabriel, Jesus, and God.

Something was pulling me, sucking me down. It was more like a pull, then tug, then, powerful drag, then massive suction. Inside my head was exploding. The watery noise—the deep, scary gurgling noise. My eardrums exploding.

I continued to fast-tumble, swim-tumble, spin, careen, hurtle. I went down even further, but not of my own volition. Spinning, tumbling, out of control. I could not control myself; I could not stop! I was like a bedraggled ship in the stormy night, rudderless, without any sails, the terrified captain, long gone, abandoned ship—rather the ship snatched from his control—and in this case spinning, tossing, being pulled and tugged, downward, to—only the heavens knew where!

Tumbling, yelling. I was in a free fall; in a tunnel, as if I was being sucked and dragged, by some gigantic and mysterious watery monster. I could feel my head about to explode. I had no idea how long I was under, or how far I had gone. No longer able to swim or maintain my balance, I abandoned all efforts at swimming, fighting.

Like a helpless rag doll, buffeted by the gurgling whooshing exploding sounds, I just tumbled and hurtled to, what I was certain was my watery, bottomless end. The thought. That scary, mind-numbing thought. It came back to me. It came back and bounced and rattled around in my head at the worst possible moment: *"You do know, the Blue Hole has NO bottom!"*

CHAPTER 7

A STRANGE WORLD COMES TO LIFE

WHEN I AWOKE—OPENED my eyes—I was on a beach. At first, I was relieved. Yes, familiar sounds! That gentle sound of waves crashing onto the shore. I laid there, waiting for the sweet cool breeze, the sound of the hysterical seagulls. However, none came. What was this place, I had stumbled—rather, tumbled onto?

However, my silent and premature elation soon faded. I had no idea where I was. Something felt strangely odd, out of place. No piercing sunlight, no ferocious rays pelting and stinging my back, not even a sound or the sight of a single bird. This beach was deserted. Where were the people, the kids kicking and splashing through the waves? Where were the women and children, hauling shads or the men scaling and gutting their catch down by the waters' edge, as the seagulls squawked and tried to attack each other over the scraps?

Maybe, I thought, it was because of my sad state, having swallowed so much dirty, bilgy water, my ears feeling completely clogged.

My head felt swollen—and it was throbbing. My poor limbs—they were flopping around in the shallow waters liked two beach something or the other. Did they even work anymore? Were they broken? They just felt loose and tired and flopped from side to side in the shallow waters. Every muscle inside my slender body ached, pulsated.

Buried halfway in sand and seaweed, I was coughing, spitting up and spewing seaweed and little tiny unidentifiable creatures out of my mouth. I tried to raise my head. Slowly. Blinking to regain full consciousness. I squinted and peered around me at the strange place that had found me.

I knew I was on a beach, because I could hear the surf and the waves crashing onto the shore, that all too familiar steady drumbeat. Where was this place? What beach? Could it be Kemps Bay, or, the more rocky beach in Smith's Hill?

My vision, coming back into focus, I thought I had better take inventory of what I knew. I realized that I was on a beach. However, it was like no other beach I had ever seen or imagined. It certainly wasn't the beach in Kemps Bay!

How did I know? Everything was black! Like it had all faded to black. Not pitch-black—just covered, enveloped in that strange eerie sort of blackness. Like those days in Andros when all of the dark clouds would unite in earnest purpose, roll collectively in, converge together in the afternoon sky, embrace, overlap, and drape everything like a thick dark blanket, a sure sign of something ominous taking place in the heavens, maybe, an approaching storm. It was like on those dark days where it would become so dark, and the rain and storm threatened, but never made good on their promise. It would be so dark and ominous-looking that all of the animals and birds would run for cover, and people, passing each other, hurrying in from their fields, balancing dexterously bundles of sugar cane or brambles for the fire on their heads would look at each other in quiet disbelief and shrug, not knowing what it all meant or portend. My dad, sitting on the porch with my mom listening to the evening news on their transistor radio, the most eventful part of their day, would look at her and say, "Hon, I think we better go in. It looks like it's about to get real nasty!"

This lonely, dreary world—this sad and black world—was what I had tumbled and tripped into—except that the darkness enveloping this world was no pretense, no bad weather rolling, barreling in, or threatening. This was its dark, sad, and depressing reality.

It was a long, lonely, curvy, stretch of beach. It *looked* like the beach in Kemps' Bay, except, rather than gleaming, glistening white sand, and sparkling, shimmering water, this beach was dark, the sand like the ash or the soot from a volcano or an earthquake. The rocks, down at the far end were also covered in the same dark sootiness. Even the seaweed—that seemed like it had been there forever—was all black and grey. The few straggly reeds and trees were all that same sooty, sickly pale grey, too. Everything hung still, limp, and lifeless. A pale smoky fog was the only thing that hung in the air and that resembled life. Everything gave off an air that there may have recently been a massive volcanic eruption or earthquake, and black sooty molten ash had just bubbled up, over-flowed, and covered the landscape.

At the end of the beach, as far as I could see, the dark sand—kind of slid, disappeared into a rocky stretch of beach. Here the rocky patches outweighed the beachy areas but were just as strangely and hauntingly beautiful. The panoramic view, if it were not for the near blackness, could be beautiful, as well. I struggled and rolled over onto my back. The sky was cloudy, dark and dreary too. There was no sign of sun, only a sickly, pale blob almost completely covered by a puffy dark mass of clouds. It looked as if it was about to rain. However, the clouds, for as long as I peered at them, did not move once.

Still feeling disoriented, I laid there, supine on my face in the sand. (I had rolled back onto my stomach—just letting my head flop back down for a minute to rest). The waves, loud, like slow but incessant drumbeats, were crashing onto the shore and over me. I was exhausted as if I had just run ten miles helter-skelter. The weight of the long perilous journey must have really taken its toll on my puny and scrawny body. It must have also been quite a long journey.

However, the only recollection my mind would confirm, because it all happened so fast, was tumbling, hurtling, and hearing a distant voice calling, yelling, "Help! Help! Somebody, help me, please—I am drowning!"

I just laid there for a moment, trying to catch my breath. Then, slowly, I propped myself up on my elbows and arms, dragged myself to my feet. I felt wobbly and the world was slowly turning and spinning this way and that. I had to get a better view. I was determined to see, look around at my strange new surroundings, at this mysterious dark, depressing, new world that had discovered me. There were no signs of life anywhere. No sounds, except the drumbeats of the wave resounding as they crashed onto the shore. *And there were no signs of my friends!*

I looked further up the beach, away from the ocean and the waves crashing onto the shore, toward where one would expect to see life. All I could see, off in the distance, were long rows of what looked like small boats, canoes, empty and ghostly looking, hauled up on the beach. They looked like an odd collection, a naval fleet, just waiting to be "commissioned" and "launched." The oars were tiny bits of driftwood, sticking out from the sides, like the many stocky legs of centipedes.

Shielding my eyes, even though there were no sun, I looked up the beach over the dark stretches of sand dunes. Scattered, what looked like, dead coconut trees, their limbs hanging limply, trailed off into the distance. These ones were not dancing to any slow, breezy, melodic beat, however. Scattered also, for some distance, as far as my eyes could see, were dark sooty shrubs, what looked like coco plum bushes, grape trees, prickly grass and long, slender reeds. These reeds were not singing and whistling. A sickly-looking type of soot coated everything. Some of the trees, standing still in the stale air, were draped with old blackened, tattered and torn, fishing nets. They looked like they had been around for hundreds of years.

Off in the distance, nestled among some of the dead coconut trees, I could make out clumsy, staggered rows of several hundred small, grey, thatched huts. They were old and they squat on the ground like giant dirty cockroaches. There were no signs of life anywhere; everything was just ghostly and scarily quiet. In the center, and somewhat removed from the others, was a slightly more imposing structure. Who lived there, I wondered? The huts had thatched roofs, covered with what looked like old dark, dusty, crusty coconut straws. All of the roofs were black with soot. They had no windows or hinges that would allow them to flap open or shut. Not that it mattered in the hot, stale, unmoving air. All of the houses looked like they were still under some sort of construction. They all just sat there, somber and grey.

There are those times when you say to yourself, *"You'd better stop, turn around, go back; run, exactly the way you came."* This was one of those times—and it wasn't! It can be hard to explain. All I knew was that my feet and legs would not let me turn around or go back. I walked slowly and carefully, trudging through the boggy sand, and in the direction of the sad looking huts. All was quiet. Too quiet! The kind of quiet that you knew—you could feel it—something was amiss, dead wrong. No birds. No seagulls, hawking and squawking hysterically. No children playing in the sand or chasing after each other or splashing in the shallows. Nothing. Just a quiet dead calm.

I pressed on, curious as to where this indistinct path would lead me. I had this strange notion I was entering enemy's territory, though there was not a single soul in sight. Instinctively, my guards went up. Slowly turning this way and that, to cover my back just in case I came under attack. Without even realizing it, I had clenched my fists, raised both arms, advancing, one slow, careful step at a time much like a courageous, but terrified fighter bracing for a fight.

Gripped by fear, I was ready to fight, or run—whichever became most necessary. Someone, once said, courage is not the absence of fear, but taking action, summoning, willing, calling on something deep within, pressing forward, in spite of our fears. Boy, did I believe them now!

Trudging up the beach away from the sea, through the boggy sand, I had come to the edge of a yard, or compound. At the entrance to the clearing, I passed under what looked like a couple of clotheslines. Draped across, and hanging limply from these "clothesline," however, were strings and strings of dried up, rotten fish. Bonefish, shads, grouper, muttonfish, hogfish, snapper, what looked like yeller tails, conch, crawfish tails, even turbits and hangies. The only fish I did not see was the revered—and much to be revered—rockfish. The array of fish on the lines seemed like they had been there a very long time. Surprisingly, too, no flies were hovering or buzzing about.

I turned my attention to the yard—or rather large compound. Looking around, all throughout the place, I could see dozens and dozens of poles, some standing up straight, and some leaning, sticking up out of the dark, sandy ground. Stuck to the top of the sticks, some pierced through, were, what looked like, barked and shucked dried coconuts. Then I noticed that there were piles of these "dried shucked coconuts" everywhere, in corners of the large compound, barely visible, some neatly stacked up against coconut trees and under coca plum bushes. Some even adorning the branches of bushes.

You somehow get use to your eyes playing tricks on you. Accept it, and move on. However, there are those times when the tricks become hauntingly real, spring to life, leaving you with nothing else to except but, "Well, Mudda sick!" This was not just one of those times—*this was a classic!*

For, as I came closer, I stopped abruptly, almost fainted. I froze! Then, I let out what was a loud sharp, peel of a scream that should have shot out like a cannon and resounded, a scream that should have woken the dead—if there were any. But my scream got halfway out of my windpipe, became trapped in my throat like a giant guenep seed that had gotten stuck. That was when I realized that those "dried shucked coconuts," were not coconuts at all—they were actually dead, decomposed human skulls! I felt sick to my stomach, doubled over, retching and clutching at air. I felt faint. My mind started racing again and my head was spinning like a top.

I screamed, "Help! Help! Somebody help me please!" My own voice just mocked me, *"Help! Help! Somebody help me please!"*

I wanted to run. Deeply agitated, immobilized with fright, confused, troubled and bewildered, it was as if I was transfixed, unable to turn or run back down the dark beach. I had never seen anything like this in all my born, natural days. Yet, no one had to tell me—I just knew—that I had stumbled, fallen, into a strange, dark, sick world, one that I could not, and would ever be able to escape from.

Time, and time again, I called out for my friends, walking, skittishly now, turning this way and that, yelling out their names, yelling at the top of my lungs, yelling until the veins were popping out my face. I yelled until it hurt to yell. I yelled the way our parents yelled, like how when we were at one end of the settlement, a half a mile away, and they wanted to reach us to tell us it was time to come home.

"Picewell-l-l-l!

Tony-y-y-y!

Lawrence-e-e-e!"

Again, just the echo of my own voice boomeranging back to me. A million thoughts were racing through my mind. The world inside my head was an alarming clutter and clatter of jumbled, confusing, and conflicting thoughts. My parents' words came floating, hauntingly, back to me:

"*Stay away!*"

"*Everybody knows it's not safe!*"

"*Stay away!*"

"*Don't even go near it!*"

"*And If I ever catch you going even near that place!*"

It was much too late for that now.

This place had a distinct mood, an oppressive one, a mood that was overwhelming like a dark, hot, oppressive air. It terrified me and sent warm chills up and down my spine.

Yes, there was something about this place! Something that was baffling, something that was just not right. It was scary and strange. Yet, in a weird, even stranger sort of way, it had a peaceful and bewitching quality to it.

This sad and dreary place, all of a sudden, reminded me of a story I had read—*The Last of the Pirates.* In that story, a group of pirates had shipwrecked on a deserted island. Stranded on that deserted island, they lived there divorced from all civilization, for over three hundred years. They set up their own crude type of government and lived by their own set of laws. Over time, they resorted to gross abuses of all description—even cannibalism.

I was deep in thoughts, thinking about all of this when… when…through the corner of my eye, I saw *something!* Or—at least—I thought I saw something! I actually thought I saw *something move!* Either it moved—or it didn't. The mind. There it goes again! In conflict with me, and itself. It either happened, or didn't. Which was it? Could it have been just a mirage? Maybe, it was just my imagination, my mind playing an insidious, cruel trick on me.

Wait! Again …it …someone …something moved! The movement that either was or wasn't had moved again! It was no mirage—and my mind was not playing tricks on me.

I tried to calm myself, steady myself, and push fear back from the front of my mind. For a moment—just for a fleeting moment—I was still prepared to try, try to convince myself that it was just my imagination, my mind playing a trick on me again. Then, it happened again!

Unmistakably! Almost imperceptible! The slightest of movement! It was human movement, just a slight shuffle, if that. Rising. That was when I tried to run, leave as fast as I could, but I was glued to the sand, paralyzed, incapable of turning or fleeing. The sand had become molasses to my feet, the gluey substance that would give a little, but held my feet firmly connected to the ground!

Shielding my eyes, even though dark clouds covered the sun, I gazed, unwilling to believe what I was seeing. One slowly rising coconut-shaped head turned into two . . . and then three . . . six . . . a dozen! Then dozens more coconut-size heads started slowly popping up from everywhere—from behind the bushes, from behind coco plum bushes, from behind clusters of dark grey sea-grapes, from behind dead coconut trees, among the long, slender reeds! The look of them were enough to make me wretch. What in the world, I thought I heard myself say! For they were old, old—real old—tired and sickly-looking, an army of ghoulish men. There must have been hundreds, if not thousands, of them, scantily clad, bows and arrows drawn, each one carrying some type of crude spear. Tied to their waists, were quivers filled with more arrows. They had strapped to their sides, also, what looked like clumsily hewn rock knives or daggers. They were armed and menacing-looking. Their grey hair and mustache—much to my utter amazement— swept the ground and the grey sooty tops of the shrubs as they moved, stealthily. They were masses of flabby arms, arms that jiggled slightly as they stood. Armed with bows and arrows, they rose slowly, very slowly like in slow motion, calculatingly. The strange world had come to life! Their bows and arrows were all drawn. Their arrows…all…were aiming straight at me!

CHAPTER 8

THE STRANGE UNDERWORLD AND ALL OF ITS INHABITANTS

WHO WAS IT that said if you always do the right thing you will live to have no regrets? Furthermore, who was it that said you should always listen to sound advice? What is more, who was it that said parents are always right? These questions were not ones that weighed on me right now. My only question—my only thought—was, who were these strange, tired-looking, old, and wizened creatures, and where did they come from?

All of them were old and flabby men—no women or children. At first sight, they looked less like humans than brown, slender, dusty creatures. They were old, shriveled up, with long unkempt, matted, grey hair and beards that reached the ground. Something else I noticed as they rose—they all had long, curled up fingernails and toenails that looked like octopus' tentacles or tangled up snakes that writhed and made a squeaky, hissing, sound as they walked. They looked like men that that even time had forgotten.

They advanced slowly, carefully, deliberately, toward me. It was like a march of spirits. It was as if they had been disturbed from a long, agonizing sleep. It looked like at any moment, they could trip on their beards. As afraid as I was, they too, seemed quite skittish. They did not seem to trust the fact that I did not trust them. After all, I guessed, I *had* disturbed them from some long, painful, distressing, and tormenting slumber.

To them, it was clear that I was an intruder. Their wild and wily looks said it all. Who are you? You are a stranger! And not just a stranger—an unwelcomed stranger, at that. They were simply responding to being disturbed from what seemed a long, unfulfilling, restive, sleep.

Clearly, my presence was unwelcomed, and they felt as if they were under attack. They advanced, cautiously, ever so slowly, as if we were all participating in some weird, ancient type of dance. They advanced closer. Slowly. Slowly closer! Closer still. This took it seemed, forever. Slowly, and methodically they encircled me, as if I were a lone fish, a stray shad or bonefish, and they, a human net. Slowly, they surrounded me, had me completely cornered and ensnared.

I struggled to remain calm, take stock of the situation. I could try to struggle. Resist. Fight back. However, from the looks of things, any attempt on my part to free myself from this tight human enclosure, seemed utterly hopeless and futile. I did struggle, tried to resist. However, all of my efforts just worked against me. After a few valiant attempts to break free, slam myself up against the flabby human wall, pounding, and throwing myself up against a few loose and wrinkled chests, I gave up and collapsed onto the dark, dusty sand.

From where I sat uncomfortably and fuming in the dirt, I peered at my captors through the corner of my eye like the caged animal I was. It was hard just to get pass their looks. Again, they were weathered and withered, as if they had been here for a long time, if not hundreds of years. They had miraculously survived—even thrived. How? I did not know, or couldn't have imagined. Etched on their faces, it seemed, were stories of a time long ago, of suffering, unspeakable pain, torture, and misery. Indeed, they seemed to live in perpetual agony and anguish as if it was some form of sustenance, some strange bush medicine. Still, there was something impressive about them—their manner, their bearing. They seemed to live by a different set of rules, rules they held to be right.

They motioned to me mutely. I could tell they wanted me to go with them. They did not speak, just kept motioning, gesticulating, with their hands. Some of them still had their weapons drawn, still trained directly on me.

All was silent. It all felt like a dream, one of those dreams that felt tortuously long, and you could not, for the life of you, wrest yourself out of it. I rubbed my eyes, blinked, and tried shutting them down, tight.

My brief dance, struggle, and capture by my captors made me think of the sand crabs again, the ones that would scamper across the sand in fear for their lives. They were little whitish-greyish creatures that scurried up and down the beach, and they built neat little burrows in the sand for themselves. I remembered how these crabs had this uncanny ability to protect themselves to "shield" themselves from attack. Whenever they would see an attacker coming, they would camouflage themselves. Then they would get into a very tight tuck position, a neat ball, cringe, and shut their eyes down tight, tight. They felt that if they couldn't see you, then you not there. I wished that I had that same uncanny ability. I tried to shut my eyes tight—even blinked a few times—to see if my strange-looking captors might go away. Much to my dismay, I met with no success, no such luck.

Once they had cornered me, sealed off all avenues of escape, they led me to a hut, the largest of the greyish huts I had seen from the beach. It was clear—because they made it resolutely clear—that I had no choice but to go with them. This hut, the largest of them all, was well swept and orderly by their standards. To me, it was a cluttered museum of artifacts—a collection of sea creatures that had died in a transfixed state, glaring and baring their teeth. Strewn all over the interior were whales, dolphins, green turtles, stingrays, wahoo, tarpons, blue marlins, sharks, some with the sucker fish still attached, barracudas, hogfish, angel fish, rock fish, blow fish, even a few hangies. Strangely enough, as my captors forcibly escorted me into the middle of the hut, and, as I looked timidly around, all of the sea creatures—all of them—seemed to be staring right at me.

The few pieces of furnishings in the hut consisted of large, use-to-be beautiful coral fans, the kind we use to brush up against when we went swimming or snorkeling on the reef right on the other side of the Tongue of the Ocean. Adorning the walls of the hut, these gigantic coral fans, carefully arranged among clusters of reef corals that still gave off the natural feel and look of the ocean. Driftwood or large chunks of dead camalame and lignum whitae logs, could be seen throughout the dark, spooky-looking hut.

Once they had pulled, half dragged me inside the dark hut, they manhandled me down onto the floor, not rough, but not friendly either.

What happened next caught me completely by surprise. My mouth wide open, I stared, as an even older, more wizened and shriveled up creature strode confidently and majestically into the room. Looking like a thin and emaciated Abraham or Moses, he carried a rod or a staff. He entered with a flourish and a stir. You could tell he was somebody important. My first thought was that he must be the prime minister or the governor general of this morbid bunch. We found out later that he was their chief. He, too, looked tired, sad, and beleaguered, a long scowl smeared across his sallow face.

Like the others, the chief's fingernails and toenails were long, and curled-up like the tentacles of an octopus, and as he walked, his fingers and toes writhed menacingly like snakes. It was hard to believe this was happening—my capture, and now, my standing before this ancient bearded, much revered one.

The chief had entered through a doorway draped with a curtain of seashells, the same shells my mom would have us collect from down by the seashore to adorn the beautiful and decorative hats and baskets she made. When the ancient-looking one entered, the silence was broken as the curtain rattled and shook. He, too, was scantily clad, except that he had an old, tattered velvet-red cloak slung loosely over his bony shoulders. A crown of what looked like a plume of coral fins and a branch of corals sat precariously on top of his head.

The chief, an emaciated, yet authoritative-looking figure, strode slowly into the slightly dark room. The chief's white mustache and beard hung limply down in front of him, sweeping the dusty floor as he walked. As he walked, his mass of fingernails and toenails, like octopus' tentacles, writhed like dark, grey snakes.

The chief looked to be about three to four hundred years old, not a day younger. In his hand, he clutched a long slender pole, what looked—from the manner in which he carried it—like a kingly scepter. At the sight of which, I almost retched again. I leaned back in horror. The sickness to my stomach that I had experienced earlier as I made my way up from the beach across the compound came flooding back. Impaled at the top of the ominous scepter was another decomposed human skull!

As scary as it was, the sight of his staff—or scepter—soon got lost in all of the strange, almost comical pomp and pageantry that would follow. All of the commotion and attention to detail was like the changing of the guard at Government House. It also reminded me of a scene from the story, King Arthur's Court. Except that in this strange, dark world, so far removed from anything we could call civilization, it all looked rather comical.

The old, wizened chief tapped with his one-of-a-kind scepter. The head atop the pole rattled and jiggled. All the other wizened and shriveled up creatures took a seat on the dark, dusty, and sandy floor. The chief tapped twice; the wizened, withered, wrinkled ones folded their arms. Then he tapped three more times and they all crossed their legs.

Now, it was all beginning to look like the convening of a political convention. However, we were quite happy and relieved when they all crossed their legs, because those skimpy pieces of loincloth they were wearing and the smell of their armpits were becoming downright embarrassing and oppressive.

The chief gave a series of loud taps with his ominous scepter. The impaled head that sat atop it shook and dangled precariously.

As I sat waiting—waiting for what, I did not know—I felt alone! Desperately alone. Part of it had to do with my new hostage environment, partly because my friends had been surreptitiously, yanked from me back in the blue hole. All I could do was sit on the dry, dusty, dark sand and fret about what was certain to be a most uncomfortable and painful end. The Heads. In my mind's eye, all I could see were the sickening, lifeless, sockets-for-eyes and sallow bony, cheekbone heads. The scalp-less heads. The piles and piles of DEAD and decomposed human skulls that greeted me when I entered the dusty, smoky compound, that adorned the place, came—along with that now familiar sickening, gut-wrenching feeling to my stomach—flooding back. The heads! Just the thought of mine tossed upon one of those unremarkable heaps, like early morning trash, only added to my deep-seated state of depression. My own scalp started to twitch, tingle, and itch.

In the middle of my musing, ruminating—call it reflecting, call it whatever you will—much to my utter amazement—my three friends, their eyes still bulging from fright and shock, were ushered—not roughly, but not friendly, either—through the inner doorway, into the large room, rattling wildly the seashell curtain once again. They looked haggard, bewildered, and in a daze. Like me, they too, must have thought they were in the middle of a nightmarish dream. Tears were streaming down my friends' cheeks. Their knees were shaking and knocking so hard, I could almost hear them from where I sat limply and dejectedly on the dark, sandy floor. The heads … Had they seen the sickly piles of head too?

They—the strange, ghostly-looking, ghoulish creatures—had tied my friends' hands tightly behind their backs with some sort of reed.

I wanted to go to them, maybe try to console them—or, better yet, for us to console each other—but a set of grimy, long fingernails pressed down on my shoulder, digging deep into my flesh, causing me to wince with pain. I took that as a warning that I had better remain calmly seated.

The chief, with much aplomb and charisma, ceremoniously raised his ominous scepter, waved it from side to side, slowly, like a sergeant of arms, and back at my friends. His voice—the first time any of them spoke—rang out like garrulous thunder, rattled throughout the hut, and rolled and floated through the coconut trees, bouncing of the tops of the coca plum bushes out onto the bay, and barreled down the dark deserted beach.

To our utter amazement, he spoke perfect Queen's English, taking pains to pronounce and enunciate all of his vowels—and his consonants. In a voice that peeled like thunder, he shouted in a loud voice, "Loose them, and let them go!"

Several sad-looking creatures untied my friends, brought them, and plunked them down on the dark sand beside me. We were too frightened to look at or even acknowledge one another. Not knowing what to expect, or what we had gotten ourselves into, we were too afraid to incite any outburst, any rebuke.

Who were these creatures? Where had they come from? Were they centuries-old survivors from a different world—our world? Were they somebody's ancestors, occupiers of the land before us? Or, were they a lost and death-defying lot that even time had forgotten or want nothing to do with. Clearly, they had aged, but life for them, had not materialized into the sure, steady slide to death!

The chief paced the length of the dark sandy floor, clutching his ominous scepter, inspecting us, looking us up and down. Then, stopping suddenly, after a great deal of pacing, he shouted, his voice, like thunder in a barrel, splitting the air, crackling and rolling down the dark and ominous-looking beach.

"What do you want? Why did you come down here? Where are you from, and who sent you?

The chief, obviously, had as many questions as we did. The ominous head atop the scepter nodded in agreement to everything the chief had to say.

Not knowing what to say, *we* kept quiet. In the predicament we were in, how could we say to him, tell him the story—which was really no stohry: *"Sir, Your Honor . . . I mean, Your Highness, Your Majesty . . . I mean, Your Right Honorable, Sir, we are just a couple of willfully disobedient kids who just wanted to go swimming in the blue hole. And we had ventured there, you see—against our wise and sage old parents' advice—and . . . while we were playing, you see—playing an innocent game of hide-and-seek, Your Holiness, we were sucked in and down in the most awful way by this quiet, yet loud, long WHOOOSH and dragged all the way down here!"*

The booming voice of the chief interrupted my thoughts. At each sound of his voice, my friends and I would lean back partly from fright, partly from the loud, thunderous sound of his voice reverberating down the lonely, dark beach.

"Answer me, I say! What made you come down here? Why did you come?" Why did you come to disturb us?

Again, none of us spoke. Had nothing to say. Did not understand the purport of the questions. Even if we wanted to speak, there was no guarantee sounds would escape our dried and parched throats and mouths. Furthermore, we all had seen the strange, sickly ornaments that adorned the trees and the bushes in the large compound. We wanted to do nothing to hasten our fate.

The chief slowly lowered himself into his seat. Even the act of sitting down, was executed ceremoniously and with a flourish. The crowd of miserable-looking minions let out an admiring gasp at the chief just taking a seat. At every word from their chief, they grunted in agreement. Then, on cue, they clapped their hands furiously, their flabby sickly-looking arms jiggling and making slapping sounds. The chief, obviously was also their king, how he had risen in rank was something we could only ponder.

The chief's throne was a dug-out chunk of driftwood. His armrests, two dead, dried-up Hammer Head sharks, their teeth still protruding glaringly and menacingly. They, too, seemed to be staring straight at me.

CHAPTER 9

EVERYBODY HAS A STORY, INCLUDING THE CHIEF!

THE CHIEF GATHERED himself slowly, officiously. Then came a long, ranting, and rambling speech from the Throne.

The chief recounted for us, slowly, sadly, the wide, sweeping history of his people. He began by saying how they were a Great Creator-fearing, seafaring, and fearless warrior-people—in-dominatable spirits. He repeated the "in-dominatable" part several times as he clenched and pumped the ghastly scepter in his hand. It was as if it were his favorite word, favorite, even if not apt description of him and his people. As the chief spoke, the precariously dangling head spun and rattled but inexplicably did not careen off its perch.

The chief said that he and his people were a proud, brave, and prosperous people before what he referred to as The Invasion and The

Devastation, two closely related events that they still celebrate in much mourning and sadness. He stated—sadly—that he and his people just wanted to live their lives in peace, in harmony with the Great Creator, all others, and the world of spirits around them.

The chief demonstrated with a wide sweeping motion of his flabby arms—he had carefully placed the scepter between his legs and now the ghastly head was looking away from me, down on the ground.

The chief said, "We thought they had come for us. We thought they were our long-lost family members, come from afar to be reacquainted after all these many, many moons! We thought that the Great Creator had brought them, guided them, and led them across the treacherous, dark, blue seas! We thought there would a celebration! We were looking forward to a celebration of life—and how life, no matter how long it takes, always triumph over loss and death. A giant celebration!

"After all these moons, to be reunited! We had welcomed them with open arms and tears streaming down our cheeks. We were willing to share—and we did share—our very selves with them. After all, we were family, One Family— long-lost family, separated only by time and space.

"Our ancestors had prepared us for this day. They had told us that, in the coming many, many moons, the Great Creator was going to reunite all the many families together again, Our ancestors had never lied to us before. Their stories were stories of veracity, handed down faithfully from generation to generation. They had never lied to us *before*. We knew that their every word could be trusted. So we had no reason to not trust them now.

"Between our ancestors' assurances, the trust we had in them, and the order that the Great Creator had instilled in all things, we made the simple mistake of daring to do what was right. We allowed ourselves to become vulnerable.

"Instead of coming to reunite hearts and souls with us, they had come—it seems, now—chasing the elusive and sacred fruits—the fruits above ground and the fruits beneath the grounds, fruits carefully placed there by Our Great Creator and imbued with his eternal spirit. What they did not know—they didn't ask us, you see—but, what they did not know was, you abuse the fruits in nature, and you release a sperit—not the spirit—no, no, not the spirit, but the sperit—of drunken greed. Once the sperit goes forth, it unleashes all the other sperits, human passions, covetousness, and greed.

"And we thought they had come for us!"

The chief was at this point grief-stricken. To be clear, more grief-stricken than before, because it seemed like they all wore the countenance of perpetual grief, longing, lost, and suffering.

The chief also noticed that he had our attention. Yes, we were transfixed—transfixed as in scared stiff, lost for words, full of questions, and bewilderment.

He continued: "Another thing about them—which we could not understand—they took a lot of interest in our features. How different we were from them. Something that did not interest us. Our ancestors had taught us that when that day came, all men would be judged not by the color of his or skin, but by the content of their character. We always knew the tiny differences you can see pale in comparison to the sameness, the oneness we cannot see.

"They became fixated in what it is they saw and dwelled on how we were *different* from them, and the staring and poking, and the nonstop staring turned into something else, something ugly!

"The staring and the leering—this is what we remembered the most. The glaring and the ebbing of respect, like how high tide turn into low tide, exposing all of the rocks and ugly parts of the beach. The making fun off. The jeering and the laughing until all of the mayhem just turned into a sense of mastery and aloofness. We could sense their sense of other, our other. Our lower—and their higher.

Then came that stale air of smugness and bossiness. They somehow owned the truth and relegated our truths to the trash heap of their forgetfulness.

"Oh, the rejection! The rejection of all that we were, all that had shaped us and our world, all that defined us. Ugliness slid into hate; hate slid into abuse."

Two of the old, withered creatures had come to attend to the chief, now. They needed to steady him, swipe at the tears as they flowed freely down his cheek. The chief remonstrated and bickered. He wanted to go on.

"They said it was nothing personal—all business. That was a new one to us—business!" They said somebody had to get their hands dirty, somebody had to stand in the hot sun, and somebody had to harvest the fruits.

"Then the abuse turned to blindness. We thought they were happy to see us. Blindness to not seeing us, not hearing us, to not even considering us. This thing that we shared, that we all had on the inside of us, somehow, got lost in translation, it seemed like. When they just stop seeing the resemblance, that was when we came to realize that we were in danger of losing the one thing that made us—and them—one, intertwined. And so, that is how the reduction happened, how we became puny, a speck in their eyes. Our ancestors had not warned us about this part the reduction. In their eyes. So we became nothing in their eyes.

"We sank. They rose. They were right and we were wrong, and so this was how they set out to sway us, swing us, to own us, to change us, our sordidness—our errors of ways, to cause our collective knees to buckle.

"Alas, our "long-lost family members" had become our enemies, and our entire world just felt like it had capsized like an attacked and overburdened canoe.

"As painful as all of this was to our collective consciousness many of my people were resigned to the spiritual defeat, they just gave up, their spirits just wilted and died to resignation."

It became too late. Almost too late for me and my people. Like the sun sinking in the west. They, too, had become blind. Blind to deceit and trickery, blind to their ways, their true intent which seemed to be the aim all along, from the beginning, from the moment they set foot ashore.

"Then they discovered the fruits in the giant rocks, fruits that shone and glistened through the rocks, the glistening breadcrumbs that led them to more fruits, fruits that sent them into a frenzy.

"They forced us to dig out the glistening fruits. They also forced us to grow and harvest other fruits in the ground. Sugar cane, cassava, yams, sweet potata, pigeon peas, coconut, guava, gueneps, scallop plums, dilly, and hog plums. To them, it was as if they had discovered a land rich beyond compare.

"That was when we decided that we had to fight! Plundering the fruits was one thing, laying down our innermost selves at their feet was too much of a sacrifice, a sacrifice we could never accept. We had reached that point where death in life for my people and I, would be the ultimate victory over an empty, deprived, and depraved life."

Huddled where we were, on the uncomfortable, irritating dark sand, it dawned on us that, in life, we all had a story. We all had a story of pain, struggle, and human survival. And the chief sure 'nough had a story to tell!

CHAPTER 10

SOMETIMES, EVEN THE SPEECH FROM THE THRONE TAKES A COMMERCIAL BREAK!

AFTER A LONG pause—the chief was shaking convulsively, now, and so too were the aids who had come alongside of him to render comfort and support.

Finally, the chief managed to steady himself enough to continue. He spoke at great length, digressing into much details, about what life was like for him and his people before the disruption and the upheaval, the coming of those he and his people thought were long-lost family members.

"All . . . all . . . all of the land above was our home!" We lived in peace—I mean—we lived in relative peace in so far as it depended on us.

"Yes, there were a few skirmishes, here and there between us, but nothing to speak off—small, little brush fires—nothing like what would be unleashed on us like when they descended the ones we thought were our long-lost family members."

The chief continued: "We always gave back to the Great Creator the hearts with the spirit of the warriors. Not the head! The head is not so tasty—except for the heads of shads, grunts, schoolie, hogfish, and grouper. Even the heads of crawfish are not good for consumption. They cause too much colic and indigestion."

The chief had much to say about their Great Creator who lived beyond the watery blue canopy above and who was aware of all of man's actions. It was clear to us that, by the term "man," the chief meant something that was both external and internal, and something that lived on into another lifetime, a second life. The term could also be applied as a plural, as in "mankind."

"The Great Creator did not mean for any man to rule over the spirit of other men. The Great Creator meant for man, those that He created in his image to be caretakers and givers. The Great creator did not mean for man, at any time, no, not ever, to be takers."

"We are supposed to give! We are supposed to be imitators. We are to care for, care for all things that the Great Creator has left in our care. We are caretakers and we are givers! That's it!"

With this, the chief would violently brush his hands off, one hand brushing off the other as if brushing off dust or filth, much like the elders of our settlement would do.

"Each person has something to give. My people were all caretakers of the land and sea! We gave and blessed the land. We blessed and gave to each other. We did not dare disturb the land. Why make the land—the spirit of the Great Creator that lives in everything—angry? Why juke up His vexation?"

From the looks of it, the chief was juking up his own vexation. He was becoming more and more agitated as he spoke. Once in a while, the motion of his wildly gesticulating hands would fan the dead and decomposed skull atop his scepter, and the head would spin and bob before coming to rest again.

The chief spoke of the "many, many, many" moons he and his people had lived ever so peacefully, like the calmness of the sea. The chief, to indicate time and the passing of time, spoke in terms of "moons." Each moon, we gathered, could indicate a century or more, but a half moon or quarter moon could mean as little as months or years.

The chief also spoke in terms of history being trustworthy and sacred, something that his ancestors had shared often and with fidelity from one generation to the next. They had done this mostly through stories as they camped around roaring, blazing fires roasting corn, cassavas and sweet potatoes and broiled fish in coconut oil on the white sandy beaches. The coconut oil, the chief said, came from the abundance of coconuts that they plucked and gathered every morning from the coconut trees that veiled the land and extended all along the eastern shores.

History, to him and his people, was an unbroken chain of events extending all the way back to the original place of human habitat, a place they called Pangeaangelos. In a section Pangeaangelos, the chief's unbroken historical record handed down from the first generation to his, recorded that in a section of Pangeaangelos, somewhere to the east, was Afracongolese, the birthplace of the family of humans. This was the birthplace of all humans, they believed. The chief was insistent that when it comes to the family of man, it all began as one and in this place.

"We all come from the one," he said.

"Our ancestors told us that much like the tree, and the trunk of the tree, life flowed from the one. First, there was a man by the name of Noahawelldeserving. Noahawelldeserving was the first, the trunk of all the families. He had several sons, three of whom were Hamladicum, Shemalodicum, and Jaffolodicum. Hamladicum was the darkest of the sons—he had dark complexion—because while the Noahawelldeserving family were still in Afracongolese, after the breakup of Pangeaangelos, Hamladicom use to stay out in the sun a lot. Shemalodicum was of a lighter complexion—he stayed indoors with his mother and read many clay tablets about exploration and adventure. Shemalodicum was of a reddish complexion—kind of like the dust from the ground. No one could explain Shemalodicum's strange complexion, other than the fact that he wandered from place to place and had gotten caught in many wind and dust storms."

"However, life flowed from the one!" The chief would repeat this refrain many times.

"And our ancestors were keen to tell us that—they were wise and had intuition, you see—whether we prosper or perish on the chunks of land we all ended up on, live or die, it all depended on us living, seeing ourselves—as we were and are—the one family!

"You see," he pointed out, "the family of man—as they grew in numbers and branched—scattered, out over what used to be Pangeaangelos—except that it is all fragmented now—would become wiser and more ignorant at the same time."

"Knowledge is something like a tool," he surmised. "You can use it to construct a beautiful hut, or you can put it to destructive ends, tearing down the many huts."

"My ancestors did tell us, that Man would come to this fork in the pathway, one of these days—and they would be armed with the most powerful, yet destructive tools."

The people on these various chunks of land, he said, his people believe, were their near to next kinfolk. However, he believed that time and the different diverse places that people drifted to had, unmistakably, and like everything else, changed large groups of his family. However, he believed that no matter where they ended up, and no matter how different their nostrils, hair, or pigmentations were, they would always, at least until the Great Creator returned, still be family.

"You see, what they did not understand is that the Great Creator, right after He had created all of everything, set about to create the one family to rule over all that He had so carefully call forth, placed and arrange. The Great Creator had to create another One Family after the first one came to the first fork in the road and used his tool to enable his own destruction."

Over time, he said, the many different families' languages and ways of life changed, but that all of them, regardless of which chunk of land they landed on, shared an incurable, indivisible, and indestructible something-that-is-hard-to-explain, put in words."

We were mesmerized, enthralled, by the veracity and philosophical, long-reaching trajectory of the chief's story. It filled us up with a certain nostalgia and appreciation for the little we knew of our own sketchy, much erased past. His compelling story almost brought tears to our eyes, almost made us forget our own serious and awful predicament.

The chief and his people had lived on the Small Islands scattered throughout the Wide Sea. His people, he said, lived in peace for many, many, long moons. They lived off the land and the sea, thriving on divine fruits such as fish, conch, crawfish, and periwinkles they would catch in the Wide Sea and scrape from along the jagged coastal rocks. They also set traps for the scrumptious white-crowned pigeons, wood-doves, and tobacco doves. The Wide Sea and the Big Dark Blue Sea with its gigantic tongue, in conjunction with the land, had provided for them all their needs.

"When we first laid eyes on them, we were overjoyed, elated! To our eyes, they looked like a blessing sent directly from the side of Our Great Creator. We thought we were about to have a grand old family reunion, a grand old family reunion with one walloping shindig on the beach. Our ancestors had told us about an eventual meeting, a time when all of the families scattered all over the earth would come together in peace, love, and harmony.

"Again, we mistook the strangers for gods, gods that had traveled across the Big, Dark-Blue Sea. We thought this because, upon first inspection, the strangers appeared to be half man and half creatures, you see. Then we came to realize that the top half of the god-like creatures could somehow, and sometime, detach itself from the bottom half. That was when we realized that the new arrivals were not gods or some strange creatures, but men just like us, men who had come and brought some animals with them. One particular animal—perhaps the most useful of everything that they brought—which they deftly mounted and rode, jostling up and down like nothing we had ever seen before.

"The strange men had pale, pinkish skins, skins that glowed in the hot sun and turned reddish like roasted crawfish the longer they stayed out in the sun. My people and I eventually concluded that the strangers were men just like us. It was just that they had a slightly different complexion from us, a lighter, paler complexion. The skin tone was never a problem for us, though, because we knew that time and location, as our wise old ancestors had taught us, change many things. However, this is what first led to us calling them "Ourpaleeabros."

"At first, we all comingled peacefully and respectfully. The spirit, the Man inside and between us, felt so right! We felt that the Great Creator had been gracious to us, had been merciful to let us see our long-lost family members again, that He had blessed us, indeed, He had let His smile shine with favor upon us!

"We showered them with gifts. Yellow golden fruits and silver fruits that would glisten in the sun, other fruits as well—seashells, tomatoes, pawpaw, sapa dillies, sour sops, sugar cane, hug plums, and cocoa beans. They showered us with fruits of their own, articles of clothing and many small trinkets. To us, it was just one big coombya!

Ourpaleeabros, interestingly enough, he and his people noticed, would not let them hold or handle the long shiny knives or the short stubby spears that spat fire. Those, they were not allowed to touch, just admire from a distance.

"Then one day, shortly after their arrival, Ourpaleeabros discovered more of the shiny fruits in the giant rocks and boulders in the backadabush. My people and I noticed that even the countenance of Ourpaleeabros began to change. Ourpaleeabros then forced us to dig out the bright, shiny, yellow fruit and the white glistening fruit and, later, forced us to work from sun up and 'til sun down in large open spaces growing all kinds of crops, which they would load onto their big canoes and head off back across the big dark-blue sea.

Oh, those were some terrible, terrible days! We did not see it coming, and we were completely taken aback by this sudden twist and turn of events.

"We remember those terrible times all too well. Terrible! Terrible! When one group of Ourpaleeabros would leave to go back with their big canoes laden with the fruits of the land, soon after, others would come. Each time they left and returned, they brought more and more Ourpaleeabroses with them. The newer arrivals were excited beyond words. They hooted and hollered, tossing their hats into the air, and seemed full of anticipation—an intoxication—to leave their big canoes and jump into the shallow clear crystal blue waters."

The chief pointed out that, he and his people, however, did not take too kindly to how Ourpaleeabros, especially the newer arrivals, started to behave. All of a sudden, the Ourpaleeabroses who had come across the dark blue yonder started acting as if they were the lords and masters and he and his people, their slaves. This arrangement, he wagged his index finger and admonished, was alien to them, and he believed, it was never even imagined nor whispered anywhere by the Great Creator.

"This was when the painful and protracted reign of terror began," the chief said. "Ourpaleeabros just started spraying, spraying us with fire from their short and stubby spears and attacking us with long shiny knives—the ones they kept half-concealed under their dresses.

"Some of his people—the ones living on the Big Islands—fled to the big rocks and into the thick, wet canopy of trees. But some of us stood our grounds, prepared to fight even if it meant giving back our spirit to our Great Creator. However, the fire-spouting short and stubby spears and the long shiny knives Ourpaleeabros kept concealed beneath their dresses were quite daunting for us."

"Our Great Creator above the watery blue knows, if it were not for the long shiny knives that flashed and glistened in the bright sunlight, the crude-looking spears that spat fire, and a strange mysterious substance that Ourpaleeabros deceitfully slipped into our water sources, *we would have prevailed, we would have been victorious in the long and protracted struggle.*

"We fought valiantly! We knew we had them outnumbered, you see. We fought valiantly, with all of the strength the Great Creator gave us—and gives us. However, when Ourpaleeabros realized that they were about to be defeated by our brave and heroic warriors, they deceitfully slipped some kind of mysterious substance into the water. This strange substance—only the Great Creator knows what it was—started causing my people to drop down dead like flies. More of my people died from the invisible deadly substance that Ourpaleeabros slipped into the water than died from the short, stubby spears that spat fire and the long skinny, shiny knives."

The chief was convinced that, if it were not for the mysterious "only-the Great Creator-knows-what" that Ourpaleeabros slipped into the water, he and his people would have snatched victory from out the very jaws of death.

Then came the most riveting part of the chief's story! The chief recounted how he and those of his people who survived the onslaught of the mysterious poison that was slipped into the water, had no other recourse available to them other than to pray to The Great Creator above the watery canopy, who also went by the name of "Hawa Great Protector." Hawa Great Protector, he said, miraculously and instantaneously caused many mouths to pop open on the belly of at least 700 of the smaller islands, hatches of escape. He and his people could choose any of the more than 150 mouths to jump into and escape the onslaught by Ourpaleeabros.

They had thought that these mouths, once they had made good their escape, would slammed back shut.

At this point, tears were streaming down the chief's face. The crowd of shriveled up followers seated on the dark, dusty sand cried and boohooed loudly, mainly from the sight of their much revered and beloved leader boohaaing.. The two wizened, old attendants were spilling tears now, too.

The chief was finally able to continue. According to him, on the belly of the largest of the islands where he and his people lived, call Androsima, more mouths popped open than anywhere else. He said, even in the midst of all the sadness, the popping open of the mouths was an amazing thing to see and hear. The sound, he said, was pulsating, like the spanking of drums. These mouths, according to the chief, just started popping open. Finally, when most all of his people had suffered an ill-fated demise, he and his clan, the remnants, he called them, escaped down the biggest hatch on Androsima's belly. Thus, they escaped to their current place, Troolydownunder.

The chief paused. He paused for a long time. He shook convulsively from remembering. His head raised slowly and sadly. Looking directly at us he muttered, "I just don't understand."

"I just don't understand," he repeated slowly, shaking his head in disbelief.

"I don't understand how those who are supposed to be family—One Family—could find it in their hearts to pillage, destroy, and vanquish like that.

The chief moaned. Sucked his teeth. He and his people, he said—the few that escaped down the mouth on Androsima's belly, had been in a suspended state of dejection, sorrow, and bewilderment ever since. It had aged them but had not attacked their indomitable will to live. The spirit in them, he said fed them and kept them alive. However, the event had made them distrustful of others. They had concluded that a new spirit of selfishness, greed, and callousness, had reared up its ugly head, had washed over all man, obliterating, sadly, he said, the strong and unmistakable resemblance we all shared. This spirit—which, the chief said was more like a sperit—now ruled in the hearts all man.

He paused—again—for what seemed like a very long time. Then he said, with a painful tinge of extra sadness in his voice, "Now, you have come. Perhaps, the Great Creator will reveal to us what we are to do in your case.

"You are clearly not one of them. You seem more like us, he said. We can still remember the hot sunny days in the land above the sea, and the discoloration and tightening of our skins, the longer we stayed out in the warm sun. Now we must wait for an answer as to what to do with you. The Great Creator always answer us in our dreams.

"Furthermore," he said, "You remind us of a time long ago, in the land above, when the sounds of women and children were like the music of the wind and the trees and the seagulls to our ears. All of our women and children perished in the long churning watery journey. It was too much for them. It became their grave, their passage to the Other Side. May the Great Creator have mercy on their cores! Your coming, as you may have seen, was very upsetting and emotionally tumultuous for us. We are still deeply torn and troubled as to what to do with you. Maybe, the Great Creator will answer in a dream this night."

We were all praying for the chief to have sweet, pleasant dreams that night. The mounds and piles of ominous ornaments piled high throughout the compound had not receded completely from our minds. From time to time, and in between the chief's Brotherhood of Man speech, they had come rushing back to us like waves crashing onto the shore.

Just before he left to go sleep, the chief muttered—his head, hung low, weighed down no doubt by the enormity of the moment—that maybe he would have a final decision for us by morning.

CHAPTER 11

THE MYSTERIOUS UNDERWORLD SAYS GOODBYE IN THE MOST UNUSUAL WAY

AT LEAST ONE of us could sleep well that night. After the chief had left to go to bed, we could not sleep a lick. Between all the wild speculations and trepidations as to what would be our fate, and the chords biting into our arms and legs, none of us could sleep. (They had fastened our hands and feet again at bedtime, maybe for fear that we might try to escape.) We tossed and turned, thinking about all of those ominous decorations adorning the poles, the trees, and the yard outside.

When the next morning finally arrived, four of them came quietly and stealthily toward us. They were not carrying any bows and arrows, we noticed. But why come to us so early in the morning, before, what we perceived, was the break of dawn?

They came, crept, up to where we were, quietly and stealthily. They shook us gruffly and untied our feet and hands. They motioned for us to come quickly. They pulled, tugged, and jostled us out of the hut and into the compound. Where were they taking us? Why had they aroused us so early in the morning?

As we came to the center of the compound, and just before we had to dodge under the clothesline with the wide array of dried rotten fish, we stopped, almost in unison.

Our sullen minders announced that the chief had decided that we be allowed to return to wherever it was we had come from. We sighed a deep sigh of relief. My friends and I cast one last glance back at the scattered rows of dark, sooty huts. The chief sat in the window of his bigger, slightly more luxurious hut. He was shaking convulsively and leaning on an elbow. At the sight of his uncontrollable grief, we almost felt sorry about our abrupt departure.

The chief had wormed his way into our hearts with his powerful Brotherhood of Man speech. In a strange way, his poignant, solemn had changed us. However, our old and wizened minders made sure we had no more adventurous ideas, or thoughts. They pulled and jerked us back around, causing us to run and skid down the rest of the dark beach.

We cast one last furtive farewell glance back at the heaps of dead, decomposed, human skulls, not sorry, in the slightest, to see them recede from view.

Our sad-looking, yet focused companions, pushed-shoved us across and down the last stretch of dark smoky-looking, hard, damp beach and into the warm shallow waters. It was all business with them, we could tell. The only time they let go of us was when we were chest deep in the calm, warm waters. Then our four aged and shriveled old handlers motioned for us to inhale and exhale deeply seven times. They made us do it a couple of times until we all got it right. This part of our journey, apparently, had to go off without a hitch. Then they told us to cover our noses with our hands. They beckoned to us, and together, we swam out into deeper waters.

The water was warm and calm. All was still, like those quiet Saturday mornings when my dad would take us fishing. I wondered what did it looked like down, below. Were the colorful fans waving? Were there a variety of colorful rocks and corals with their beautiful and intricate designs? and were the fish—just as colorful and varied—darting to and fro? However, this was no time to be daydreaming now.

When we were far out into the deep, our withered and flabby escorts motioned for us to stop. They instructed us to once again inhale and exhale deeply seven times. What's with the seven times, I wondered? We swam farther out to sea, still. I could not help thinking how lucky we were how lucky we were; we all knew how to swim. Our age-old, shriveled companions swam well, too, for their age, their droopy skins floating on the surface of the water like the dark, brown wings of old stingrays. After a third intermission, where we inhaled and exhaled deeply seven more times, we went on one last swim, stroking and striding noisily in the calm of the morning. Then we came to an area where it was bubbling and gurgling, spinning and churning, like a whirlwind, and we heard that unmistakable whooshing sound again. It sucked us in, and we went spinning round and round, sucked in by the swooshing rapid currents of water. Something, like a blow from a blunt object, struck me upside my head. Stars danced before my eyes, and I lost all consciousness.

The next thing I knew we were back in the now all to familiar blue hole, splashing, coughing, choking loudly, spitting up water, and trying to catch our breaths. The waters of the blue hole did not feel quite so cool and refreshing anymore.

The four ageless and tired-looking companions escorted us back into the settlement. Strangely, they seemed to know the way. Had they been here before?

A few of our friends—the ones who were much smarter than we were—and a few of our relatives lined the main road and gawked at us as if we were the dead, come back to life. We walked in silence, like a couple of sullen and beleaguered prisoners on a sad parade. The broken line of people that lined the street stared unbelievingly at us. Their mouths hang open. Some covered their mouths with their hand and whispered to one another. They were too confused and frightened to ask us where we had been, or who were our strange, ancient-looking companions with beards that swept the street and long finger nails and toenails that looked like octopus' tentacles, or snakes, that writhed when they walked and made a sickening hissing sound. We could see, from the movements of their lips, half concealed behind their cupped hands, our relatives, Cousin So and So, were more than curious about our four other-worldly companions.

We walked on. The ghoulish, ancient creatures seemed to be quite familiar with their surroundings, as if it were somewhere they had seen before. At one point they stopped, looked east, then west, north, and then south. They sniffed the air, took deep long draughts, relishing, for a moment, the crisp and, to them, balmy air. They took a few more deep long breaths. It was as if they had sorely missed breathing the fresh salty air. When I had stolen a quick glance at one of them, I could have sworn that he was tearing up.

As we walked deeper into the heart of the settlement, they stared long and hard at the coconut trees, swaying gently in the cool breeze. They could not get enough of the fresh, clean air, the brilliant gleam of the sunlight. We were all squinting, having difficulties readjusting again to the bright, piercing sunlight.

Our four sad-looking companions shielded their eyes and squinted for a long time. I could tell that they were deeply moved by their surroundings—the noisy, smoky and corn roasting, dogs barking, chickens clucking, and the sounds of laughter and excited children in the street and in the Crossroad. Some were playing stickball with old stuffed socks. Others were playing cars, steering their tireless tire-less bicycle wheel rims with sticks and self-fashioned old clothes hangers.

Suddenly, it was as if our two strange "companions" snapped to, remembering the seriousness of their journey, that they were on a solemn mission. That stern look we had become accustomed to, returned to their faces. We walked on, resolutely. It was if they did not see the onlookers anymore, our Cousin So and So, This One and That one.

Fortunately, for our gruff companions, all of our parents were huddled together at my house, consoling, or trying to console one another. They had no doubt thought they had seen the last of us. Did they know that we had gone swimming in the blue hole?

When our parents saw us, they let out a collective gasp. Shock, horror, and glee all mingled together and registered on their faces. Our sad-looking friends just walked right in, almost as if they owned the place. Some brave soul muttered softly under their breath that our ancient-looking companions "may as well just take a seat." The men said no, they could not tarry. They had come only to deliver a message. From the stern looks that had returned to their faces, we could almost guess what that message would be. The message was from their chief.

Our parents all leaned forward, almost in unison, straining to receive and digest all they had to say.

One of the men stepped forward. The chief, he said, after much heartburns, colicky stomach, and deliberations, had decided to spare us, allow us to return to our homes and to be with our parents again. The chief did not want to cause our parents any more grief, colickiness, or heartburns. However, he was returning us with a solemn warning. The message was brusque and straight to the point.

"Keep your boys away from the blue hole! If they were *ever* to return to the blue hole, you would never see or hear from them again!"

gaulins: Type of dusty-grey, long-necked cranes found in the Bahamas

"Dick and Jane": Euro-centric children stories popular in the Bahamas and elsewhere in the 1960s and early 70s.

Spot: Dog character in the "Dick and Jane" books

Nassau: Small capital city of the Bahamas; known for its hustle and bustle lifestyle

bay: Androsians (Bahamians on the Bahamian island of Andros) typically use this word in reference to the beach

Paulting (pelting): To throw stones (specifically at an object)

The Drain: A distinctive place in South Andros, a natural inland spring

"fixed": As in under a spell, relating to witchcraft or voodoo

"pot-cake": Nick name for a type of stray dog in the Bahamas, known for its aggressiveness

"chim-chims": Name given to all small birds by kids on Andros Island

rockfish: A type of shoal fish known to be poisonous

stohry: a lie

sperit: another word for spirit, especially an evil, haunting spirit

"juke up" one's vexation: to become angry or very emotional

Wide Sea: The Caribbean Sea

Big Dark Blue Sea: Atlantic Ocean

"colicky" stomach: Upset stomach

www.ingramcontent.com/pod-product-compliance
Lightning Source LLC
Chambersburg PA
CBHW060805210726
48292CB00013B/1764